"I am the giant Skrymir."
[Frontispiece]
See page 86.

FAVORITE NORSE MYTHS

ABBIE FARWELL BROWN

WITH THE ORIGINAL ILLUSTRATIONS BY
E. BOYD SMITH

DOVER PUBLICATIONS, INC.
MINEOLA, NEW YORK

Bibliographical Note

This Dover edition, first published in 2006, is an unabridged republication of the work originally published as *In the Days of Giants: A Book of Norse Tales* by Houghton, Mifflin and Co., Boston and New York, in 1906.

Library of Congress Cataloging-in-Publication Data

Brown, Abbie Farwell, d. 1927.
   [In the days of giants]
   Favorite Norse myths / Abbie Farwell Brown ; with original illustrations by E. Boyd Smith.
     p. cm.
   Originally published: In the days of giants. Boston ; New York : Houghton Mifflin and Co., 1902.
   ISBN-13: 978-0-486-45119-0 (pbk.)
   ISBN 0-486-45119-4 (pbk.)
   1. Mythology, Norse. I. Smith, E. Boyd (Elmer Boyd), 1860–1943.
II. Title.
   BL860.B76 2006
   398.2'09363—dc22

                                     2006040281

Manufactured in the United States by Courier Corporation
45119402   2013
www.doverpublications.com

Now I like a really good saga, about gods and giants, and the fire kingdoms, and the snow kingdoms, and the Æsir making men and women out of two sticks, and all that.

Kingsley's *Hypatia*

Contents

PAGE

I. The Beginning of Things 1

II. How Odin Lost His Eye 6

III. Kvasir's Blood 12

IV. The Giant Builder 20

V. The Magic Apples 28

VI. Skadi's Choice 40

VII. The Dwarf's Gifts 46

VIII. Loki's Children 57

IX. The Quest of the Hammer 63

X. The Giantess Who Would Not 76

XI. Thor's Visit to the Giants 84

XII. Thor's Fishing 98

XIII. Thor's Duel 109

XIV. In the Giant's House 118

XV. Balder and the Mistletoe 128

XVI. The Punishment of Loki 139

Illustrations

PAGE

"I am the giant Skrymir." (page 86)   *Frontispiece*

He flapped away with her, magic apples
   and all 35

The third gift—an enormous hammer. 51

"Ah, what a lovely maid it is!" 69

Each arrow overshot his head. 131

"Kill him! Kill him!" 147

Favorite Norse Myths

The Beginning of Things

The oldest stories of every race of people tell about the Beginning of Things. But the various folk who first told them were so very different, the tales are so very old, and have changed so greatly in the telling from one generation to another, that there are almost as many accounts of the way in which the world began as there are nations upon the earth. So it is not strange that the people of the North have a legend of the Beginning quite different from that of the Southern, Eastern, and Western folk.

This book is made of the stories told by the Northern folk,—the people who live in the land of the midnight sun, where summer is green and pleasant, but winter is a terrible time of cold and gloom; where rocky mountains tower like huge giants, over whose heads the thunder rolls and crashes, and under whose feet are mines of precious metals. Therefore you will find the tales full of giants and dwarfs,—spirits of the cold mountains and dark caverns.

You will find the hero to be Thor, with his thunderbolt hammer, who dwells in the happy heaven of Asgard, where All-Father Odin is king, and where Balder the beautiful makes springtime with his smile. In the north countries, winter, cold, and frost are very real and terrible enemies; while spring, sunshine, and warmth are near and dear friends. So the story of the Beginning of Things is a story of cold and heat, of the wicked giants who loved the cold, and of the good Æsir, who basked in pleasant warmth.

In the very beginning of things, the stories say, there were two worlds, one of burning heat and one of icy cold.

The cold world was in the north, and from it flowed Elivâgar, a river of poisonous water which hardened into ice and piled up into great mountains, filling the space which had no bottom. The other world in the south was on fire with bright flame, a place of heat most terrible. And in those days through all space there was nothing beside these two worlds of heat and cold.

But then began a fierce combat. Heat and cold met and strove to destroy each other, as they have tried to do ever since. Flaming sparks from the hot world fell upon the ice river which flowed from the place of cold. And though the bright sparks were quenched, in dying they wrought mischief, as they do to-day; for they melted the ice, which dripped and dripped, like tears from the suffering world of cold. And then, wonderful to say, these chilly drops became alive; became a huge, breathing mass, a Frost-Giant with a wicked heart of ice. And he was the ancestor of all the giants who came afterwards, a bad and cruel race.

At that time there was no earth nor sea nor heaven, nothing but the icy abyss without bottom, whence Ymir the giant had sprung. And there he lived, nourished by the milk of a cow which the heat had formed. Now the cow had nothing for her food but the snow and ice of Elivâgar, and that was cold victuals indeed! One day she was licking the icy rocks, which tasted salty to her, when Ymir noticed that the mass was taking a strange shape. The more the cow licked it, the plainer became the outline of the shape. And when evening came Ymir saw thrusting itself through the icy rock a head of hair. The next day the cow went on with her meal, and at night-time a man's head appeared above the rock. On the third day the cow licked away the ice until forth stepped a man, tall and powerful and handsome. This was no evil giant, for he was good; and, strangely, though he came from the ice his heart was warm. He was the ancestor of the kind Æsir; for All-Father Odin and his brothers Vili and Ve, the first of the gods, were his grandsons, and as soon as they were born they became the enemies of the race of giants.

Now after a few giant years,—ages and ages of time as

we reckon it,—there was a great battle, for Odin and his brothers wished to destroy all the evil in the world and to leave only good. They attacked the wicked giant Ymir, first of all his race, and after hard fighting slew him. Ymir was so huge that when he died a mighty river of blood flowed from the wounds which Odin had given him; a stream so large that it flooded all space, and the frost-giants, his children and grandchildren, were drowned, except one who escaped with his wife in a chest. And but for the saving of these two, that would have been the end of the race of giants.

All-Father and his brothers now had work to do. Painfully they dragged the great bulk of Ymir into the bottomless space of ice, and from it they built the earth, the sea, and the heavens. Not an atom of his body went to waste. His blood made the great ocean, the rivers, lakes, and springs. His mighty bones became mountains. His teeth and broken bones made sand and pebbles. From his skull they fashioned the arching heaven, which they set up over the earth and sea. His brain became the heavy clouds. His hair sprouted into trees, grass, plants, and flowers. And last of all, the Æsir set his bristling eyebrows as a high fence around the earth, to keep the giants away from the race of men whom they had planned to create for this pleasant globe.

So the earth was made. And next the gods brought light for the heavens. They caught the sparks and cinders blown from the world of heat, and set them here and there, above and below, as sun and moon and stars. To each they gave its name and told what its duties were to be, and how it must perform them, day after day, and year after year, and century after century, till the ending of all things; so that the children of men might reckon time without mistake.

Sôl and Mâni, who drove the bright chariots of the sun and moon across the sky, were a fair sister and brother whose father named them Sun and Moon because they were so beautiful. So Odin gave them each a pair of swift, bright horses to drive, and set them in the sky forever. Once upon a time,—but that was many, many years later,— Mâni, the Man in the Moon, stole two children from the earth. Hiuki and Bil were going to a well to draw a pail of water. The little boy and girl carried a pole and a bucket across their shoulders, and looked so pretty that Mâni thrust down a long arm and snatched them up to his moon. And there they are to this day, as you can see on any moon-light night,—two little black shadows on the moon's bright face, the boy and the girl, with the bucket between them.

The gods also made Day and Night. Day was fair, bright, and beautiful, for he was of the warm-hearted Æsir race. But Night was dark and gloomy, because she was one of the cold giant-folk. Day and Night had each a chariot drawn by a swift horse, and each in turn drove about the world in a twenty-four hours' journey. Night rode first behind her dark horse, Hrîmfaxi, who scattered dew from his bit upon the sleeping earth. After her came Day with his beautiful horse, Glad, whose shining mane shot rays of light through the sky.

All these wonders the kind gods wrought that they might make a pleasant world for men to call their home. And now the gods, or Æsir as they were called, must choose a place for their own dwelling, for there were many of them, a glori-ous family. Outside of everything, beyond the great ocean which surrounded the world, was Jotunheim, the cold coun-try where the giants lived. The green earth was made for men. The gods therefore decided to build their city above men in the heavens, where they could watch the doings of their favorites and protect them from the wicked giants. Asgard was to be their city, and from Asgard to Midgard, the home of men, stretched a wonderful bridge, a bridge of many colors. For it was the rainbow that we know and love. Up and down the rainbow bridge the Æsir could travel to the earth, and thus keep close to the doings of men.

Next, from the remnants of Ymir's body the gods made the race of little dwarfs, a wise folk and skillful, but in nature more like the giants than like the good Æsir; for they were spiteful and often wicked, and they loved the dark and the cold better than light and warmth. They lived deep down below the ground in caves and rocky dens, and it was their business to dig the precious metals and glittering gems that were hidden in the rocks, and to make wonderful things from the treasures of the underworld. Pouf! pouf! went their little bellows. Tink-tank! went their little hammers on their little anvils all day and all night. Sometimes they were friendly to the giants, and sometimes they did kindly deeds for the Æsir. But always after men came upon the earth they hated these new folk who eagerly sought for the gold and the jewels which the dwarfs kept hidden in the ground. The dwarfs lost no chance of doing evil to the race of men.

Now the gods were ready for the making of men. They longed to have a race of creatures whom they could love and protect and bless with all kinds of pleasures. So Odin, with his brothers Hœnir and Loki, crossed the rainbow bridge and came down to the earth. They were walking along the seashore when they found two trees, an ash and an elm. These would do as well as anything for their purpose. Odin took the two trees and warmly breathed upon them; and lo! they were alive, a man and a woman. Hœnir then gently touched their foreheads, and they became wise. Lastly Loki softly stroked their faces; their skin grew pink with ruddy color, and they received the gifts of speech, hearing, and sight. Ask and Embla were their names, and the ash and the elm became the father and mother of the whole human race whose dwelling was Midgard, under the eyes of the Æsir who had made them.

This is the story of the Beginning of Things.

How Odin Lost His Eye

In the beginning of things, before there was any world or sun, moon, and stars, there were the giants; for these were the oldest creatures that ever breathed. They lived in Jotunheim, the land of frost and darkness, and their hearts were evil. Next came the gods, the good Æsir, who made earth and sky and sea, and who dwelt in Asgard, above the heavens. Then were created the queer little dwarfs, who lived underground in the caverns of the mountains, working at their mines of metal and precious stones. Last of all, the gods made men to dwell in Midgard, the good world that we know, between which and the glorious home of the Æsir stretched Bifröst, the bridge of rainbows.

In those days, folk say, there was a mighty ash-tree named Yggdrasil, so vast that its branches shaded the whole earth and stretched up into heaven where the Æsir dwelt, while its roots sank far down below the lowest depth. In the branches of the big ash-tree lived a queer family of creatures. First, there was a great eagle, who was wiser than any bird that ever lived—except the two ravens, Thought and Memory, who sat upon Father Odin's shoulders and told him the secrets which they learned in their flight over the wide world. Near the great eagle perched a hawk, and four antlered deer browsed among the buds of Yggdrasil. At the foot of the tree coiled a huge serpent, who was always gnawing hungrily at its roots, with a whole colony of little snakes to keep him company,—so many that they could never be counted. The eagle at the top of the tree and the serpent at its foot were enemies, always saying hard things of each other. Between the two skipped up and down a little squirrel, a tale-bearer and a gossip, who repeated each unkind remark and, like the malicious neighbor that he was, kept their quarrel ever fresh and green.

In one place at the roots of Yggdrasil was a fair fountain called the Urdar-well, where the three Norn-maidens, who knew the past, present, and future, dwelt with their pets, the two white swans. This was magic water in the fountain, which the Norns sprinkled every day upon the giant tree to keep it green,—water so sacred that everything which entered it became white as the film of an eggshell. Close beside this sacred well the Æsir had their council hall, to which they galloped every morning over the rainbow bridge.

But Father Odin, the king of all the Æsir, knew of another fountain more wonderful still; the two ravens whom he sent forth to bring him news had told him. This also was below the roots of Yggdrasil, in the spot where the sky and ocean met. Here for centuries and centuries the giant Mimer had sat keeping guard over his hidden well, in the bottom of which lay such a treasure of wisdom as was to be found nowhere else in the world. Every morning Mimer dipped his glittering horn Giöll into the fountain and drew out a draught of the wondrous water, which he drank to make him wise. Every day he grew wiser and wiser; and as this had been going on ever since the beginning of things, you can scarcely imagine how wise Mimer was.

Now it did not seem right to Father Odin that a giant should have all this wisdom to himself; for the giants were the enemies of the Æsir, and the wisdom which they had been hoarding for ages before the gods were made was generally used for evil purposes. Moreover, Odin longed and longed to become the wisest being in the world. So he resolved to win a draught from Mimer's well, if in any way that could be done.

One night, when the sun had set behind the mountains of Midgard, Odin put on his broad-brimmed hat and his striped cloak, and taking his famous staff in his hand, trudged down the long bridge to where it ended by Mimer's secret grotto.

"Good-day, Mimer," said Odin, entering; "I have come for a drink from your well."

The giant was sitting with his knees drawn up to his chin, his long white beard falling over his folded arms, and his head nodding; for Mimer was very old, and he often fell asleep while watching over his precious spring. He woke with a frown at Odin's words. "You want a drink from my well, do you?" he growled. "Hey! I let no one drink from my well."

"Nevertheless, you must let me have a draught from your glittering horn," insisted Odin, "and I will pay you for it."

"Oho, you will pay me for it, will you?" echoed Mimer, eyeing his visitor keenly. For now that he was wide awake, his wisdom taught him that this was no ordinary stranger. "What will you pay for a drink from my well, and why do you wish it so much?"

"I can see with my eyes all that goes on in heaven and upon earth," said Odin, "but I cannot see into the depths of ocean. I lack the hidden wisdom of the deep,—the wit that lies at the bottom of your fountain. My ravens tell me many secrets; but I would know all. And as for payment, ask what you will, and I will pledge anything in return for the draught of wisdom."

Then Mimer's keen glance grew keener. "You are Odin, of the race of gods," he cried. "We giants are centuries older than you, and our wisdom which we have treasured during these ages, when we were the only creatures in all space, is a precious thing. If I grant you a draught from my well, you will become as one of us, a wise and dangerous enemy. It is a goodly price, Odin, which I shall demand for a boon so great."

Now Odin was growing impatient for the sparkling water. "Ask your price," he frowned. "I have promised that I will pay."

"What say you, then, to leaving one of those far-seeing eyes of yours at the bottom of my well?" asked Mimer, hoping that he would refuse the bargain. "This is the only payment I will take."

Odin hesitated. It was indeed a heavy price, and one that he could ill afford, for he was proud of his noble beauty. But he glanced at the magic fountain bubbling mysteriously in the shadow, and he knew that he must have the draught.

"Give me the glittering horn," he answered. "I pledge you my eye for a draught to the brim."

Very unwillingly Mimer filled the horn from the fountain of wisdom and handed it to Odin. "Drink, then," he said; "drink and grow wise. This hour is the beginning of trouble between your race and mine." And wise Mimer foretold the truth.

Odin thought merely of the wisdom which was to be his. He seized the horn eagerly, and emptied it without delay. From that moment he became wiser than any one else in the world except Mimer himself.

Now he had the price to pay, which was not so pleasant. When he went away from the grotto, he left at the bottom of the dark pool one of his fiery eyes, which twinkled and winked up through the magic depths like the reflection of a star. This is how Odin lost his eye, and why from that day he was careful to pull his gray hat low over his face when he wanted to pass unnoticed. For by this oddity folk could easily recognize the wise lord of Asgard.

In the bright morning, when the sun rose over the mountains of Midgard, old Mimer drank from his bubbly well a draught of the wise water that flowed over Odin's pledge. Doing so, from his underground grotto he saw all that befell in heaven and on earth. So that he also was wiser by the bargain. Mimer seemed to have secured rather the best of it; for he lost nothing that he could not spare, while Odin lost what no man can well part with,—one of the good windows wherethrough his heart looks out upon the world. But there was a sequel to these doings which made the balance swing down in Odin's favor.

Not long after this, the Æsir quarreled with the Vanir, wild enemies of theirs, and there was a terrible battle. But in the end the two sides made peace; and to prove that they meant never to quarrel again, they exchanged hostages. The Vanir gave to the Æsir old Niörd the rich, the lord of the sea and the ocean wind, with his two children, Frey and Freia. This was indeed a gracious gift; for Freia was the most beautiful maid in the world, and her twin brother was almost as fair. To the Vanir in return Father Odin gave his own brother Hœnir. And with Hœnir he sent Mimer the wise, whom he took from his lonely well.

Now the Vanir made Hœnir their chief, thinking that he must be very wise because he was the brother of great Odin, who had lately become famous for his wisdom. They did not know the secret of Mimer's well, how the hoary old giant was far more wise than any one who had not quaffed of the magic water. It is true that in the assemblies of the Vanir Hœnir gave excellent counsel. But this was because Mimer whispered in Hœnir's ear all the wisdom that he uttered. Witless Hœnir was quite helpless without his aid, and did not know what to do or say. Whenever Mimer was absent he would look nervous and frightened, and if folk questioned him be always answered:—

"Yes, ah yes! Now go and consult some one else."

Of course the Vanir soon grew very angry at such silly answers from their chief, and presently they began to suspect the truth. "Odin has deceived us," they said. "He has sent us his foolish brother with a witch to tell him what to say. Ha! We will show him that we understand the trick."

So they cut off poor old Mimer's head and sent it to Odin as a present.

The tales do not say what Odin thought of the gift. Perhaps he was glad that now there was no one in the whole world who could be called so wise as himself. Perhaps he was sorry for the danger into which he had thrust a poor old giant who had never done him any wrong, except to be a giant of the race which the Æsir hated. Perhaps he was a little ashamed of the trick which he had played on the Vanir. Odin's new wisdom showed him how to prepare Mimer's head with herbs and charms, so that it stood up by itself quite naturally and seemed not dead. Thenceforth Odin kept it near him, and learned from it many useful secrets which it had not forgotten.

So in the end Odin fared better than the unhappy Mimer, whose worst fault was that he knew more than most folk. That is a dangerous fault, as others have found; though it is not one for which many of us need fear being punished.

Kvasir's Blood

Once upon a time there lived a man named Kvasir, who was so wise that no one could ask him a question to which he did not know the answer, and who was so eloquent that his words dripped from his lips like notes of music from a lute. For Kvasir was the first poet who ever lived, the first of those wise makers of songs whom the Norse folk named *skalds*. This Kvasir received his precious gifts wonderfully; for he was made by the gods and the Vanir, those two mighty races, to celebrate the peace which was evermore to be between them.

Up and down the world Kvasir traveled, lending his wisdom to the use of men, his brothers; and wherever he went he brought smiles and joy and comfort, for with his wisdom he found the cause of all men's troubles, and with his songs he healed them. This is what the poets have been doing in all the ages ever since. Folk declare that every skald has a drop of Kvasir's blood in him. This is the tale which is told to show how it happened that Kvasir's blessed skill has never been lost to the world.

There were two wicked dwarfs named Fialar and Galar who envied Kvasir his power over the hearts of men, and who plotted to destroy him. So one day they invited him to dine, and while he was there, they begged him to come aside with them, for they had a very secret question to ask, which only he could answer. Kvasir never refused to turn his wisdom to another's help; so, nothing suspecting, he went with them to hear their trouble.

12

Thereupon this sly pair of wicked dwarfs led him into a lonely corner. Treacherously they slew Kvasir; and because their cunning taught them that his blood must be precious, they saved it in three huge kettles, and mixing it with honey, made thereof a magic drink. Truly, a magic drink it was; for whoever tasted of Kvasir's blood was straightway filled with Kvasir's spirit, so that his heart taught wisdom and his lips uttered the sweetest poesy. Thus the wicked dwarfs became possessed of a wonderful treasure.

When the gods missed the silver voice of Kvasir echoing up from the world below, they were alarmed, for Kvasir was very dear to them. They inquired what had become of him, and finally the wily dwarfs answered that the good poet had been drowned in his own wisdom. But Father Odin, who had tasted another wise draught from Mimer's well, knew that this was not the truth, and kept his watchful eye upon the dark doings of Fialar and Galar.

Not long after this the dwarfs committed another wicked deed. They invited the giant Gilling to row out to sea with them, and when they were a long distance from shore, the wicked fellows upset the boat and drowned the giant, who could not swim. They rowed back to land, and told the giant's wife how the "accident" had happened. Then there were giant shrieks and howls enough to deafen all the world, for the poor giantess was heartbroken, and her grief was a giant grief. Her sobs annoyed the cruel-hearted dwarfs. So Fialar, pretending to sympathize, offered to take her where she could look upon the spot where her dear husband had last been seen. As she passed through the gateway, the other dwarf, to whom his brother had made a sign, let a huge millstone fall upon her head. That was the ending of her, poor thing, and of her sorrow, which had so disturbed the little people, crooked in heart as in body.

But punishment was in store for them. Suttung, the

huge son of Gilling, learned the story of his parents' death, and presently, in a dreadful rage, he came roaring to the home of the dwarfs. He seized one of them in each big fist, and wading far out to sea, set the wretched little fellows on a rock which at high tide would be covered with water.

"Stay there," he cried, "and drown as my father drowned!" The dwarfs screamed thereat for mercy so loudly that he had to listen before he went away.

"Only let us off, Suttung," they begged, "and you shall have the precious mead made from Kvasir's blood."

Now Suttung was very anxious to own this same mead, so at last he agreed to the bargain. He carried them back to land, and they gave him the kettles in which they had mixed the magic fluid. Suttung took them away to his cave in the mountains, and gave them in charge of his fair daughter Gunnlöd. All day and all night she watched by the precious kettles, to see that no one came to steal or taste of the mead; for Suttung thought of it as his greatest treasure, and no wonder.

Father Odin had seen all these deeds from his seat above the heavens, and his eye had followed longingly the passage of the wondrous mead, for Odin longed to have a draught of it. Odin had wisdom, he had drained that draught from the bottom of Mimer's mystic fountain; but he lacked the skill of speech which comes of drinking Kvasir's blood. He wanted the mead for himself and for his children in Asgard, and it seemed a shame that this precious treasure should be wasted upon the wicked giants who were their enemies. So he resolved to try if it might not be won in some sly way.

One day he put on his favorite disguise as a wandering old man, and set out for Giant-Land, where Suttung dwelt. By and by he came to a field where nine workmen were cutting hay. Now these were the servants of Baugi, the brother of Suttung, and this Odin knew. He walked up to the men and watched them working for a little while.

"Ho!" he exclaimed at last, "your scythes are dull. Shall

I whet them for you?" The men were glad enough to accept his offer, so Odin took a whetstone from his pocket and sharpened all the scythes most wonderfully. Then the men wanted to buy the stone; each man would have it for his own, and they fell to quarreling over it. To make matters more exciting, Odin tossed the whetstone into their midst, saying:—

"Let him have it who catches it!" Then indeed there was trouble! The men fought with one another for the stone, slashing right and left with their sharp scythes until every one was killed. Odin hastened away, and went up to the house where Baugi lived. Presently home came Baugi, complaining loudly and bitterly because his quarrelsome servants had killed one another, so that there was not one left to do his work.

"What am I going to do?" he cried. "Here it is mowing time, and I have not a single man to help me in the field!"

Then Odin spoke up. "I will help you," he said. "I am a stout fellow, and I can do the work of nine men if I am paid the price I ask."

"What is the price which you ask?" queried Baugi eagerly, for he saw that this stranger was a mighty man, and he thought that perhaps he could do as he boasted.

"I ask that you get for me a drink of Suttung's mead," Odin answered.

Then Baugi eyed him sharply. "You are one of the gods," he said, "or you would not know about the precious mead. Therefore I know that you can do my work, the work of nine men. I cannot give you the mead. It is my brother's, and he is very jealous of it, for he wishes it all himself. But if you will work for me all the summer, when winter comes I will go with you to Suttung's home and try what I can do to get a draught for you."

So they made the bargain, and all summer Father Odin worked in the fields of Baugi, doing the work of nine men. When the winter came, he demanded his pay. So then they set out for Suttung's home, which was a cave deep down in the mountains, where it seems not hard to hide one's treasures. First Baugi went to his brother and told him of the agreement between him and the stranger, begging for a gift of the magic mead wherewith to pay the stout laborer who had done the work of nine. But Suttung refused to spare even a taste of the precious liquor.

"This laborer of yours is one of the gods, our enemies," he said. "Indeed, I will not give him of the precious mead. What are you thinking of, brother!" Then he talked to Baugi till the giant was ready to forget his promise to Odin, and to desire only the death of the stranger who had come forward to help him.

Baugi returned to Odin with the news that the mead was not to be had with Suttung's consent. "Then we must get it without his consent," declared Odin. "We must use our wits to steal it from under his nose. You must help me, Baugi, for you have promised."

Baugi agreed to this; but in his heart he meant to entrap Odin to his death. Odin now took from his pocket an auger such as one uses to bore holes. "Look, now," he said. "You shall bore a hole into the roof of Suttung's cave, and when the hole is large enough, I will crawl through and get the mead."

"Very well," nodded Baugi, and he began to bore into the mountain with all his might and main. At last he cried, "There, it is done; the mountain is pierced through!" But when Odin blew into the hole to see whether it did indeed go through into the cave, the dust made by the auger flew into his face. Thus he knew that Baugi was deceiving him, and thenceforth he was on his guard, which was fortunate.

"Try again," said Odin sternly. "Bore a little deeper, friend Baugi." So Baugi went at the work once more, and this time when he said the hole was finished, Odin found that his word was true, for the dust blew through the hole and disappeared in the cave. Now Odin was ready to try the plan which he had been forming.

Odin's wisdom taught him many tricks, and among them he knew the secret of changing his form into that of any creature he chose. He turned himself into a worm,—a long, slender, wiggly worm, just small enough to be able to enter the hole that Baugi had pierced. In a moment he had thrust his head into the opening, and was wriggling out of sight before Baugi had even guessed what he meant to do. Baugi jumped forward and made a stab at him with the pointed auger, but it was too late. The worm's striped tail quivered in out of sight, and Baugi's wicked attempt was spoiled.

When Odin had crept through the hole, he found himself in a dark, damp cavern, where at first he could see nothing. He changed himself back into his own noble form, and then he began to hunt about for the kettles of magic mead. Presently he came to a little chamber, carefully hidden in a secret corner of this secret grotto,—a chamber locked and barred and bolted on the inside, so that no one could enter by the door. Suttung had never thought of such a thing as that a stranger might enter by a hole in the roof!

At the back of this tiny room stood three kettles upon the floor; and beside them, with her head resting on her elbow, sat a beautiful maiden, sound asleep. It was Gunnlöd, Suttung's daughter, the guardian of the mead. Odin stepped up to her very softly, and bending over, kissed her gently upon the forehead. Gunnlöd awoke with a start, and at first she was horrified to find a stranger in the cave where it seemed impossible that a stranger could enter. But when she saw the beauty of Odin's face and the kind look of his eye, she was no longer afraid, but glad that he had come. For poor Gunnlöd often grew lonesome in this gloomy cellar-home, where Suttung kept her prisoner day and night to watch over the three kettles.

"Dear maiden," said Odin, "I have come a long, long distance to see you. Will you not bid me stay a little while?"

Gunnlöd looked at him kindly. "Who are you, and whence do you come so far to see me?" she asked.

"I am Odin, from Asgard. The way is long and I am thirsty. Shall I not taste the liquor which you have there?"

Gunnlöd hesitated. "My father bade me never let soul taste of the mead," she said. "I am sorry for you, however, poor fellow! You look very tired and thirsty. You may have one little sip." Then Odin kissed her and thanked her, and tarried there with such pleasant words for the maiden that before he was ready to go she granted him what he asked,— three draughts, only three draughts of the mead.

Now Odin took up the first kettle to drink, and with one draught he drained the whole. He did the same by the next, and the next, till before she knew it, Gunnlöd found herself guarding three empty kettles. Odin had gained what he came for, and it was time for him to be gone before Suttung should come to seek him in the cave. He kissed fair Gunnlöd once again, with a sigh to think that he must treat her so unfairly. Then he changed himself into an eagle, and away he flew to carry the precious mead home to Asgard.

Meanwhile Baugi had told the giant Suttung how Odin the worm had pierced through into his treasure-cave; and when Suttung, who was watching, saw the great eagle fly forth, he guessed who this eagle must be. Suttung also put on an eagle's plumage, and a wonderful chase began. Whirr, whirr! The two enormous birds winged their way toward Asgard, Suttung close upon the other's flight. Over the mountains they flew, and the world was darkened as if by the passage of heavy storm-clouds, while the trees, blown by the breeze from their wings, swayed, and bent almost to the ground.

It was a close race; but Odin was the swifter of the two, and at last he had the mead safe in Asgard, where the gods were waiting with huge dishes to receive it from his mouth. Suttung was so close upon him, however, that he jostled Odin even as he was filling the last dish, and some of the mead was spilled about in every direction over the world. Men rushed from far and near to taste of these wasted drops of Kvasir's blood, and many had just enough to make them dizzy, but not enough to make them wise. These folk are the poor poets, the makers of bad verses, whom one finds to this day satisfied with their meagre, stolen portion, scattered drops of the sacred draught.

The mead that Odin had captured he gave to the gods, a wondrous gift; and they in turn cherished it as their most precious treasure. It was given into the special charge of old Bragi of the white beard, because his taste of the magic mead had made him wise and eloquent above all others. He was the sweetest singer of all the Æsir, and his speech was poetry. Sometimes Bragi gave a draught of Kvasir's blood to some favored mortal, and then he also became a great poet. He did not do this often,—only once or twice in the memory of an old man; for the precious mead must be made to last a long, long time, until the world be ready to drop to pieces, because this world without its poets would be too dreadful a place to imagine.

The Giant Builder

Ages and ages ago, when the world was first made, the gods decided to build a beautiful city high above the heavens, the most glorious and wonderful city that ever was known. Asgard was to be its name, and it was to stand on Ida Plain under the shade of Yggdrasil, the great tree whose roots were underneath the earth.

First of all they built a house with a silver roof, where there were seats for all the twelve chiefs. In the midst, and high above the rest, was the wonder-throne of Odin the All-Father, whence he could see everything that happened in the sky or on the earth or in the sea. Next they made a fair house for Queen Frigg and her lovely daughters. Then they built a smithy, with its great hammers, tongs, anvils, and bellows, where the gods could work at their favorite trade, the making of beautiful things out of gold; which they did so well that folk name that time the Golden Age. Afterwards, as they had more leisure, they built separate houses for all the Æsir, each more beautiful than the preceding, for of course they were continually growing more skillful. They saved Father Odin's palace until the last, for they meant this to be the largest and the most splendid of all.

Gladsheim, the home of joy, was the name of Odin's house, and it was built all of gold, set in the midst of a wood whereof the trees had leaves of ruddy gold,—like an autumn-gilded forest. For the safety of All-Father it was surrounded by a roaring river and by a high picket fence; and there was a great courtyard within.

The glory of Gladsheim was its wondrous hall, radiant with gold, the most lovely room that time has ever seen. Valhalla, the Hall of Heroes, was the name of it, and it was roofed with the mighty shields of warriors. The ceiling was made of interlacing spears, and there was a portal at the west end before which hung a great gray wolf, while over him a fierce eagle hovered. The hall was so huge that it had 540 gates, through each of which 800 men could march abreast. Indeed, there needed to be room, for this was the hall where every morning Odin received all the brave warriors who had died in battle on the earth below; and there were many heroes in those days.

This was the reward which the gods gave to courage. When a hero had gloriously lost his life, the Valkyries, the nine warrior daughters of Odin, brought his body up to Valhalla on their white horses that gallop the clouds. There they lived forever after in happiness, enjoying the things that they had most loved upon earth. Every morning they armed themselves and went out to fight with one another in the great courtyard. It was a wondrous game, wondrously played. No matter how often a hero was killed, he became alive again in time to return perfectly well to Valhalla, where he ate a delicious breakfast with the Æsir; while the beautiful Valkyries who had first brought him thither waited at table and poured the blessed mead, which only the immortal taste. A happy life it was for the heroes, and a happy life for all who dwelt in Asgard; for this was before trouble had come among the gods, following the mischief of Loki.

This is how the trouble began. From the beginning of time, the giants had been unfriendly to the Æsir, because the giants were older and huger and more wicked; besides, they were jealous because the good Æsir were fast gaining more wisdom and power than the giants had ever known. It was the Æsir who set the fair brother and sister, Sun and Moon, in the sky to give light to men; and it was they also who made the jeweled stars out of sparks from the place of fire. The giants hated the Æsir, and tried all in their power to injure them and the men of the earth below, whom the Æsir loved and cared for. The gods had already built a wall around Midgard, the world of men, to keep the giants out; built it of the bushy eyebrows of Ymir, the oldest and hugest of giants. Between Asgard and the giants flowed Ifing, the great river on which ice never formed, and which the gods crossed on the rainbow bridge. But this was not protection enough. Their beautiful new city needed a fortress.

So the word went forth in Asgard,—"We must build us a fortress against the giants; the hugest, strongest, finest fortress that ever was built."

Now one day, soon after they had announced this decision, there came a mighty man stalking up the rainbow bridge that led to Asgard city.

"Who goes there!" cried Heimdal the watchman, whose eyes were so keen that he could see for a hundred miles around, and whose ears were so sharp that he could hear the grass growing in the meadow and the wool on the backs of the sheep. "Who goes there! No one can enter Asgard if I say no."

"I am a builder," said the stranger, who was a huge fellow with sleeves rolled up to show the iron muscles of his arms. "I am a builder of strong towers, and I have heard that the folk of Asgard need one to help them raise a fair fortress in their city."

Heimdal looked at the stranger narrowly, for there was that about him which his sharp eyes did not like. But he made no answer, only blew on his golden horn, which was so loud that it sounded through all the world. At this signal all the Æsir came running to the rainbow bridge, from wherever they happened to be, to find out who was coming to Asgard. For it was Heimdal's duty ever to warn them of the approach of the unknown.

"This fellow says he is a builder," quoth Heimdal. "And he would fain build us a fortress in the city."

"Ay, that I would," nodded the stranger. "Look at my iron arm; look at my broad back; look at my shoulders. Am I not the workman you need?"

"Truly, he is a mighty figure," vowed Odin, looking at him approvingly. "How long will it take you alone to build our fortress? We can allow but one stranger at a time within our city, for safety's sake."

"In three half-years," replied the stranger, "I will undertake to build for you a castle so strong that not even the giants, should they swarm hither over Midgard,—not even they could enter without your leave."

"Aha!" cried Father Odin, well pleased at this offer. "And what reward do you ask, friend, for help so timely?"

The stranger hummed and hawed and pulled his long beard while he thought. Then he spoke suddenly, as if the idea had just come into his mind. "I will name my price, friends," he said; "a small price for so great a deed. I ask you to give me Freia for my wife, and those two sparkling jewels, the Sun and Moon."

At this demand the gods looked grave; for Freia was their dearest treasure. She was the most beautiful maid who ever lived, the light and life of heaven, and if she should leave Asgard, joy would go with her; while the Sun and Moon were the light and life of the Æsir's children, men, who lived in the little world below. But Loki the sly whispered that they would be safe enough if they made another condition on their part, so hard that the builder could not fulfill it. After thinking cautiously, he spoke for them all.

"Mighty man," quoth he, "we are willing to agree to your price—upon one condition. It is too long a time that you ask; we cannot wait three half-years for our castle; that is equal to three centuries when one is in a hurry. See that you finish the fort without help in one winter, one short winter, and you shall have fair Freia with the Sun and Moon. But if, on the first day of summer, one stone is wanting to the walls, or if any one has given you aid in the building, then your reward is lost, and you shall depart without payment." So spoke Loki, in the name of all the gods; but the plan was his own.

At first the stranger shook his head and frowned, saying that in so short a time no one unaided could complete the undertaking. At last he made another offer. "Let me have but my good horse to help me, and I will try," he urged. "Let me bring the useful Svadilföri with me to the task, and I will finish the work in one winter of short days, or lose my reward. Surely, you will not deny me this little help, from one four-footed friend."

Then again the Æsir consulted, and the wiser of them were doubtful whether it were best to accept the stranger's offer so strangely made. But again Loki urged them to accept. "Surely, there is no harm," he said. "Even with his old horse to help him, he cannot build the castle in the promised time. We shall gain a fortress without trouble and with never a price to pay."

Loki was so eager that, although the other Æsir did not like this crafty way of making bargains, they finally consented. Then in the presence of the heroes, with the Valkyries and Mimer's head for witnesses, the stranger and the Æsir gave solemn promise that the bargain should be kept.

On the first day of winter the strange builder began his work, and wondrous was the way he set about it. His strength seemed as the strength of a hundred men. As for his horse Svadilföri, he did more work by half than even the mighty builder. In the night he dragged the enormous rocks that were to be used in building the castle, rocks as big as mountains of the earth; while in the daytime the stranger piled them into place with his iron arms. The Æsir watched him with amazement; never was seen such strength in Asgard. Neither Týr the stout nor Thor the strong could match the power of the stranger. The gods began to look at one another uneasily. Who was this mighty one who had come among them, and what if after all he should win his reward? Freia trembled in her palace, and the Sun and Moon grew dim with fear.

Still the work went on, and the fort was piling higher and higher, by day and by night. There were but three days left before the end of winter, and already the building was so tall and so strong that it was safe from the attacks of any giant. The Æsir were delighted with their fine new castle; but their pride was dimmed by the fear that it must be paid for at all too costly a price. For only the gateway remained to be completed, and unless the stranger should fail to finish that in the next three days, they must give him Freia with the Sun and Moon.

The Æsir held a meeting upon Ida Plain, a meeting full of fear and anger. At last they realized what they had done; they had made a bargain with one of the giants, their enemies; and if he won the prize, it would mean sorrow and darkness in heaven and upon earth. "How did we happen to agree to so mad a bargain?" they asked one another. "Who suggested the wicked plan which bids fair to cost us all that we most cherish?" Then they remembered that it was Loki who had made the plan; it was he who had insisted that it be carried out; and they blamed him for all the trouble.

"It is your counsels, Loki, that have brought this danger upon us," quoth Father Odin, frowning. "You chose the way of guile, which is not our way. It now remains for you to help us by guile, if you can. But if you cannot save for us Freia and the Sun and Moon, you shall die. This is my word." All the other Æsir agreed that this was just. Thor alone was away hunting evil demons at the other end of the world, so he did not know what was going on, and what dangers were threatening Asgard.

Loki was much frightened at the word of All-Father. "It was my fault," he cried, "but how was I to know that he was a giant? He had disguised himself so that he seemed but a strong man. And as for his horse,—it looks much like that of other folk. If it were not for the horse, he could not finish the work. Ha! I have a thought! The builder shall not finish the gate; the giant shall not receive his payment. I will cheat the fellow."

Now it was the last night of winter, and there remained but a few stones to put in place on the top of the wondrous gateway. The giant was sure of his prize, and chuckled to himself as he went out with his horse to drag the remaining stones; for he did not know that the Æsir had guessed at last who he was, and that Loki was plotting to outwit him. Hardly had he gone to work when out of the wood came running a pretty little mare, who neighed to Svadilföri as if inviting the tired horse to leave his work and come to the green fields for a holiday.

Svadilföri, you must remember, had been working hard all winter, with never a sight of four-footed creature of his kind, and he was very lonesome and tired of dragging stones. Giving a snort of disobedience, off he ran after this new friend towards the grassy meadows. Off went the giant after him, howling with rage, and running for dear life, as he saw not only his horse but his chance of success slipping out of reach. It was a mad chase, and all Asgard thundered with the noise of galloping hoofs and the giant's mighty tread. The mare who raced ahead was Loki in disguise, and he led Svadilföri far out of reach, to a hidden meadow that he knew; so that the giant howled and panted up and down all night long, without catching even a sight of his horse.

Now when the morning came the gateway was still unfinished, and night and winter had ended at the same hour. The giant's time was over, and he had forfeited his reward. The Æsir came flocking to the gateway, and how they laughed and triumphed when they found three stones wanting to complete the gate!

"You have failed, fellow," judged Father Odin sternly, "and no price shall we pay for work that is still undone. You have failed. Leave Asgard quickly; we have seen all we want of you and of your race."

Then the giant knew that he was discovered, and he

was mad with rage. "It was a trick!" he bellowed, assuming his own proper form, which was huge as a mountain, and towered high beside the fortress that he had built. "It was a wicked trick. You shall pay for this in one way or another. I cannot tear down the castle which, ungrateful ones, I have built you, stronger than the strength of any giant. But I will demolish the rest of your shining city!" Indeed, he would have done so in his mighty rage; but at this moment Thor, whom Heimdal had called from the end of the earth by one blast of the golden horn, came rushing to the rescue, drawn in his chariot of goats. Thor jumped to the ground close beside the giant, and before that huge fellow knew what had happened, his head was rolling upon the ground at Father Odin's feet; for with one blow Thor had put an end to the giant's wickedness and had saved Asgard.

"This is the reward you deserve!" Thor cried. "Not Freia nor the Sun and Moon, but the death that I have in store for all the enemies of the Æsir."

In this extraordinary way the noble city of Asgard was made safe and complete by the addition of a fortress which no one, not even the giant who built it, could injure, it was so wonder-strong. But always at the top of the gate were lacking three great stones that no one was mighty enough to lift. This was a reminder to the Æsir that now they had the race of giants for their everlasting enemies. And though Loki's trick had saved them Freia, and for the world the Sun and Moon, it was the beginning of trouble in Asgard which lasted as long as Loki lived to make mischief with his guile.

The Magic Apples

It is not very amusing to be a king. Father Odin often grew tired of sitting all day long upon his golden throne in Valhalla above the heavens. He wearied of welcoming the new heroes whom the Valkyries brought him from wars upon the earth, and of watching the old heroes fight their daily deathless battles. He wearied of his wise ravens, and the constant gossip which they brought him from the four corners of the world; and he longed to escape from every one who knew him to some place where he could pass for a mere stranger, instead of the great king of the Æsir, the mightiest being in the whole universe, of whom every one was afraid.

Sometimes he longed so much that he could not bear it. Then—he would run away. He disguised himself as a tall old man, with white hair and a long gray beard. Around his shoulders he threw a huge blue cloak, that covered him from top to toe, and over his face he pulled a big slouch hat, to hide his eyes. For his eyes Odin could not change—no magician has ever learned how to do that. One was empty; he had given the eye to the giant Mimer in exchange for wisdom.

Usually Odin loved to go upon these wanderings alone; for an adventure is a double adventure when one meets it single-handed. It was a fine game for Odin to see how near he could come to danger without feeling the grip of its teeth. But sometimes, when he wanted company, he would whisper to his two brothers, Hœnir and red Loki.

They three would creep out of the palace by the back way; and, with a finger on the lip to Heimdal, the watchman, would silently steal over the rainbow bridge which led from Asgard into the places of men and dwarfs and giants.

Wonderful adventures they had, these three, with Loki to help make things happen. Loki was a sly, mischievous fellow, full of his pranks and his capers, not always kindly ones. But he was clever, as well as malicious; and when he had pushed folk into trouble, he could often help them out again, as safe as ever. He could be the jolliest of companions when he chose, and Odin liked his merriment and his witty talk.

One day Loki did something which was no mere jest nor easily forgiven, for it brought all Asgard into danger. And after that Father Odin and his children thought twice before inviting Loki to join them in any journey or undertaking. This which I am about to tell was the first really wicked deed of which Loki was found guilty, though I am sure his red beard had dabbled in secret wrongs before.

One night the three high gods, Odin, Hœnir, and Loki, stole away from Asgard in search of adventure. Over mountains and deserts, great rivers and stony places, they wandered until they grew very hungry. But there was no food to be found—not even a berry or a nut.

Oh, how footsore and tired they were! And oh, how faint! The worst of it ever is that—as you must often have noticed—the heavier one's feet grow, the lighter and more hollow becomes one's stomach; which seems a strange thing, when you think of it. If only one's feet became as light as the rest of one feels, folk could fairly fly with hunger. Alas! this is not so.

The three Æsir drooped and drooped, and seemed on the point of starving, when they came to the edge of a valley. Here, looking down, they saw a herd of oxen feeding on the grass.

"Hola!" shouted Loki. "Behold our supper!" Going down

into the valley, they caught and killed one of the oxen, and, building a great bonfire, hung up the meat to roast. Then the three sat around the fire and smacked their lips, waiting for the meat to cook. They waited for a long time.

"Surely, it is done now," said Loki, at last; and he took the meat from the fire. Strange to say, however, it was raw as ere the fire was lighted. What could it mean? Never before had meat required so long a time to roast. They made the fire brighter and re-hung the beef for a thorough basting, cooking it even longer than they had done at first. When again they came to carve the meat, they found it still uneatable. Then, indeed, they looked at one another in surprise.

"What can this mean?" cried Loki, with round eyes.

"There is some trick!" whispered Hœnir, looking around as if he expected to see a fairy or a witch meddling with the food.

"We must find out what this mystery betokens," said Odin thoughtfully. Just then there was a strange sound in the oak-tree under which they had built their fire.

"What is that?" Loki shouted, springing to his feet. They looked up into the tree, and far above in the branches, near the top, they spied an enormous eagle, who was staring down at them, and making a queer sound, as if he were laughing.

"Ho-ho!" croaked the eagle. "I know why your meat will not cook. It is all my doing, masters."

The three Æsir stared in surprise. Then Odin said sternly: "Who are you, Master Eagle? And what do you mean by those rude words?"

"Give me my share of the ox, and you shall see," rasped the eagle, in his harsh voice. "Give me my share, and you will find that your meat will cook as fast as you please."

Now the three on the ground were nearly famished. So, although it seemed very strange to be arguing with an eagle, they cried, as if in one voice: "Come down, then, and take your share." They thought that, being a mere bird, he would want but a small piece.

The eagle flapped down from the top of the tree. Dear me! What a mighty bird he was! Eight feet across the wings was the smallest measure, and his claws were as long and strong as ice-hooks. He fanned the air like a whirlwind as he flew down to perch beside the bonfire. Then in his beak and claws he seized a leg and both shoulders of the ox, and started to fly away.

"Hold, thief!" roared Loki angrily, when he saw how much the eagle was taking. "That is not your share; you are no lion, but you are taking the lion's share of our feast. Begone, Scarecrow, and leave the meat as you found it!" Thereat, seizing a pole, he struck at the eagle with all his might.

Then a strange thing happened. As the great bird flapped upward with his prey, giving a scream of malicious laughter, the pole which Loki still held stuck fast to the eagle's back, and Loki was unable to let go of the other end.

"Help, help!" he shouted to Odin and to Hœnir, as he felt himself lifted off his feet. But they could not help him. "Help, help!" he screamed, as the eagle flew with him, now high, now low, through brush and bog and briar, over tree-tops and the peaks of mountains. On and on they went, until Loki thought his arm would be pulled out, like a weed torn up by the roots. The eagle would not listen to his cries nor pause in his flight, until Loki was almost dead with pain and fatigue.

"Hark you, Loki," screamed the eagle, going a little more slowly; "no one can help you except me. You are bewitched, and you cannot pull away from this pole, nor loose the pole from me, until I choose. But if you will promise what I ask, you shall go free."

Then Loki groaned: "O eagle, only let me go, and tell me who you really are, and I will promise whatever you wish."

The eagle answered: "I am the giant Thiasse, the enemy of the Æsir. But you ought to love me, Loki, for you yourself married a giantess."

Loki moaned: "Oh, yes! I dearly love all my wife's family, great Thiasse. Tell me what you want of me?"

"I want this," quoth Thiasse gruffly. "I am growing old, and I want the apples which Idun keeps in her golden casket, to make me young again. You must get them for me."

Now these apples were the fruit of a magic tree, and were more beautiful to look at and more delicious to taste than any fruit that ever grew. The best thing about them was that whoever tasted one, be he ever so old, grew young and strong again. The apples belonged to a beautiful lady named Idun, who kept them in a golden casket. Every morning the Æsir came to her to be refreshed and made over by a bite of her precious fruit. That is why in Asgard no one ever waxed old or ugly. Even Father Odin, Hœnir, and Loki, the three travelers who had seen the very beginning of everything, when the world was made, were still sturdy and young. And so long as Idun kept her apples safe, the faces of the family who sat about the table of Valhalla would be rosy and fair like the faces of children.

"O friend giant!" cried Loki. "You know not what you ask! The apples are the most precious treasure of Asgard, and Idun keeps watch over them as if they were dearer to her than life itself. I never could steal them from her, Thiasse; for at her call all Asgard would rush to the rescue, and trouble would buzz about my ears like a hive of bees let loose."

"Then you must steal Idun herself, apples and all. For the apples I must have, and you have promised, Loki, to do my bidding."

Loki sniffed and thought, thought and sniffed again. Already his mischievous heart was planning how he might steal Idun away. He could hardly help laughing to think how angry the Æsir would be when they found their beauty-medicine gone forever. But he hoped that, when he had done this trick for Thiasse, now and then the giant would let him have a nibble of the magic apples; so that Loki himself would remain young long after the other Æsir were grown old and feeble. This thought suited Loki's malicious nature well.

"I think I can manage it for you, Thiasse," he said craftily. "In a week I promise to bring Idun and her apples to you. But you must not forget the great risk which I am running, nor that I am your relative by marriage. I may have a favor to ask in return, Thiasse."

Then the eagle gently dropped Loki from his claws. Falling on a soft bed of moss, Loki jumped up and ran back to his traveling companions, who were glad and surprised to see him again. They had feared that the eagle was carrying him away to feed his young eaglets in some far-off nest. Ah, you may be sure that Loki did not tell them who the eagle really was, nor confess the wicked promise which he had made about Idun and her apples.

After that the three went back to Asgard, for they had had adventure enough for one day.

The days flew by, and the time came when Loki must fulfill his promise to Thiasse. So one morning he strolled out into the meadow where Idun loved to roam among the flowers. There he found her, sitting by a tiny spring, and holding her precious casket of apples on her lap. She was combing her long golden hair, which fell from under a wreath of spring flowers, and she was very beautiful. Her green robe was embroidered with buds and blossoms of silk in many colors, and she wore a golden girdle about her waist. She smiled as Loki came, and tossed him a posy, saying: "Good-morrow, red Loki. Have you come for a bite of my apples? I see a wrinkle over each of your eyes which I can smooth away."

"Nay, fair lady," answered Loki politely, "I have just nibbled of another apple, which I found this morning. Verily, I think it is sweeter and more magical than yours."

Idun was hurt and surprised.

"That cannot be, Loki," she cried. "There are no apples anywhere like mine. Where found you this fine fruit?" and she wrinkled up her little nose scornfully.

"Oho! I will not tell any one the place," chuckled Loki, "except that it is not far, in a little wood. There is a gnarled old apple-tree, and on its branches grow the most beautiful red-cheeked apples you ever saw. But you could never find it."

"I should like to see these apples, Loki, if only to prove how far less good they are than mine. Will you bring me some ?"

"That I will not," said Loki teasingly. "Oh, no! I have my own magic apples now, and folk will be coming to me for help instead of to you."

Idun began to coax him, as he had guessed that she would: "Please, please, Loki, show me the place!"

At first he would not, for he was a sly fellow, and knew how to lead her on. At last, he pretended to yield.

"Well, then, because I love you, Idun, better than all the rest, I will show you the place, if you will come with me. But it must be a secret—no one must ever know."

All girls like secrets.

"Yes—yes!" cried Idun eagerly. "Let us steal away now, while no one is looking."

This was just what Loki hoped for.

"Bring your own apples," he said, "that we may compare them with mine. But I know mine are better."

"I know mine are the best in all the world," returned Idun, pouting. "I will bring them, to show you the difference."

Off they started together, she with the golden casket under her arm; and Loki chuckled wickedly as they went. He led her for some distance, further than she had ever strayed before, and at last she grew frightened.

"Where are you taking me, Loki?" she cried. "You said it was not far. I see no little wood, no old apple-tree."

"It is just beyond, just a little step beyond," he answered. So on they went. But that little step took them beyond the boundary of Asgard—just a little step beyond, into the space where the giants lurked and waited for mischief.

Then there was a rustling of wings, and *whirr-rr-rr!* Down came Thiasse in his eagle dress. Before Idun suspected what was happening, he fastened his claws into her girdle and flapped away with her, magic apples and all, to his palace in Jotunheim, the Land of Giants.

He flapped away with her,
magic apples and all.
See page 34.

Loki stole back to Asgard, thinking that he was quite safe, and that no one would discover his villainy. At first Idun was not missed. But after a little the gods began to feel signs of age, and went for their usual bite of her apples. Then they found that she had disappeared, and a great terror fell upon them. Where had she gone? Suppose she should not come back!

The hours and days went by, and still she did not return. Their fright became almost a panic. Their hair began to turn gray, and their limbs grew stiff and gouty so that they hobbled down Asgard streets. Even Freia, the loveliest, was afraid to look in her mirror, and Balder the beautiful grew pale and haggard. The happy land of Asgard was like a garden over which a burning wind had blown,—all the flower-faces were faded and withered, and springtime was turned into yellow fall.

If Idun and her apples were not quickly found, the gods seemed likely to shrivel and blow away like autumn leaves. They held a council to inquire into the matter, endeavoring to learn who had seen Idun last, and whither she had gone. It turned out that one morning Heimdal had seen her strolling out of Asgard with Loki, and no one had seen her since. Then the gods understood; Loki was the last person who had been with her—this must be one of Loki's tricks. They were filled with anger. They seized and bound Loki and brought him before the council. They threatened him with torture and with death unless he should tell the truth. And Loki was so frightened that finally he confessed what he had done.

Then indeed there was horror in Asgard. Idun stolen away by a wicked giant! Idun and her apples lost, and Asgard growing older every minute! What was to be done? Big Thor seized Loki and threw him up in the air again and again, so that his heels touched first the moon and then the sea; you can still see the marks upon the moon's white face. "If you do not bring Idun back from the land of your wicked wife, you shall have worse than this!" he roared. "Go and bring her *now*."

"How can I do that?" asked Loki, trembling.

"That is for you to find," growled Thor. "Bring her you must. Go!"

Loki thought for a moment. Then he said:—

"I will bring her back if Freia will loan me her falcon dress. The giant dresses as an eagle. I, too, must guise me as a bird, or we cannot outwit him."

Then Freia hemmed and hawed. She did not wish to loan her feather dress, for it was very precious. But all the Æsir begged; and finally she consented.

It was a beautiful great dress of brown feathers and gray, and in it Freia loved to skim like a falcon among the clouds and stars. Loki put it on, and when he had done so he looked exactly like a great brown hawk. Only his bright black eyes remained the same, glancing here and there, so that they lost sight of nothing.

With a whirr of his wings Loki flew off to the north, across mountains and valleys and the great river Ifing, which lay between Asgard and Giant Land. And at last he came to the palace of Thiasse the giant.

It happened, fortunately, that Thiasse had gone fishing in the sea, and Idun was left alone, weeping and broken-hearted. Presently she heard a little tap on her window, and, looking up, she saw a great brown bird perching on the ledge. He was so big that Idun was frightened and gave a scream. But the bird nodded pleasantly and croaked: "Don't be afraid, Idun. I am a friend. I am Loki, come to set you free."

"Loki! Loki is no friend of mine. He brought me here," she sobbed. " I don't believe you came to save me."

"That is indeed why I am here," he replied, "and a dangerous business it is, if Thiasse should come back before we start for home."

"How will you get me out?" asked Idun doubtfully. "The door is locked, and the window is barred."

"I will change you into a nut," said he, "and carry you in my claws."

"What of the casket of apples?" queried Idun. "Can you carry that also?"

Then Loki laughed long and loudly.

"What welcome to Asgard do you think I should receive without the apples?" he cried. "Yes, we must take them, indeed."

Idun came to the window, and Loki, who was a skillful magician, turned her into a nut and took her in one claw, while in the other he seized the casket of apples. Then off he whirred out of the palace grounds and away toward Asgard's safety.

In a little while Thiasse returned home, and when he found Idun and her apples gone, there was a hubbub, you may be sure! However, he lost little time by smashing mountains and breaking trees in his giant rage; that fit was soon over. He put on his eagle plumage and started in pursuit of the falcon.

Now an eagle is bigger and stronger than any other bird, and usually in a long race he can beat even the swift hawk who has an hour's start. Presently Loki heard behind him the shrill scream of a giant eagle, and his heart turned sick. But he had crossed the great river, and already was in sight of Asgard. The aged Æsir were gathered on the rainbow bridge watching eagerly for Loki's return; and when they spied the falcon with the nut and the casket in his talons, they knew who it was. A great cheer went up, but it was hushed in a moment, for they saw the eagle close after the falcon; and they guessed that this must be the giant Thiasse, the stealer of Idun.

Then there was a great shouting of commands, and a rushing to and fro. All the gods, even Father Odin and his two wise ravens, were busy gathering chips into great heaps on the walls of Asgard. As soon as Loki, with his precious burden, had fluttered weakly over the wall, dropping to the ground beyond, the gods lighted the heaps of chips which they had piled, and soon there was a wall of fire, over which the eagle must fly. He was going too fast to stop. The flames roared and crackled, but Thiasse flew straight into them, with a scream of fear and rage. His feathers caught fire and burned, so that he could no longer fly, but fell headlong to the ground inside the walls. Then Thor, the thunder-lord, and Týr, the mighty war-king, fell upon him and slew him, so that he could never trouble the Æsir any more.

There was great rejoicing in Asgard that night, for Loki changed Idun again to a fair lady; whereupon she gave each of the eager gods a bite of her life-giving fruit, so that they grew young and happy once more, as if all these horrors had never happened.

Not one of them, however, forgot the evil part which Loki had played in these doings. They hid the memory, like a buried seed, deep in their hearts. Thenceforward the word of Loki and the honor of his name were poor coin in Asgard; which is no wonder.

Skadi's Choice

The giant Thiasse, whom Thor slew for the theft of Idun and the magic apples, had a daughter, Skadi, who was a very good sort of girl, as giantesses go. Most of them were evil-tempered, spiteful, and cruel creatures, who desired only to do harm to the gods and to all who were good. But Skadi was different. Stronger than the hatred of her race for the Æsir, stronger even than her wish to be revenged for her father's death, was her love for Balder the beautiful, the pride of all the gods. If she had not been a giantess, she might have hoped that he would love her also; but she knew that no one who lived in Asgard would ever think kindly of her race, which had caused so much trouble to Balder and his brothers. After her father was killed by the Æsir, however, Skadi had a wise idea.

Skadi put on her helm and corselet and set out for Asgard, meaning to ask a noble price to pay for the sorrow of Thiasse's death. The gods, who had all grown young and boyish once again, were sitting in Valhalla merrily enjoying a banquet in honor of Idun's safe return, when Skadi, clattering with steel, strode into their midst. Heimdal the watchman, astonished at the sight, had let this maiden warrior pass him upon the rainbow bridge. The Æsir set down their cups hastily, and the laughter died upon their lips; for though she looked handsome, Skadi was a terrible figure in her silver armor and with her spear as long as a ship's mast brandished in her giant hand.

The nine Valkyries, Odin's maiden warriors, hurried away to put on their own helmets and shields; for they would not have this other maiden, ten times as huge, see them meekly waiting at table, while they had battle-dresses as fine as hers to show the stranger.

"Who are you, maiden, and what seek you here?" asked Father Odin.

"I am Skadi, the daughter of Thiasse, whom your folk have slain," answered she, "and I come here for redress."

At these words the coward Loki, who had been at the killing of Thiasse, skulked low behind the table; but Thor, who had done the killing, straightened himself and clenched his fists tightly. He was not afraid of any giant, however fierce, and this maiden with her shield and spear only angered him.

"Well, Skadi," quoth Odin gravely, "your father was a thief, and died for his sins. He stole fair Idun and her magic apples, and for that crime he died, which was only just. Yet because our righteous deed has left you an orphan, Skadi, we will grant you a recompense, so you shall be at peace with us; for it is not fitting that the Æsir should quarrel with women. What is it you ask, O Skadi, as solace for the death of Thiasse?"

Skadi looked like an orphan who was well able to take care of herself; and this indeed her next words showed her to be. "I ask two things," she said, without a moment's hesitation: "I ask the husband whom I shall select from among you; and I ask that you shall make me laugh, for it is many days since grief has let me enjoy a smile."

At this strange request the Æsir looked astonished, and some of them seemed rather startled; for you can fancy that none of them wanted a giantess, however handsome, for his wife. They put their heads together and consulted long whether or not they should allow Skadi her two wishes.

"I will agree to make her laugh," grinned Loki; "but suppose she should choose me for her husband! I am married to one giantess already."

"No fear of that, Loki," said Thor; "you were too near being the cause of her father's death for her to love you overmuch. Nor do I think that she will choose me; so I am safe."

Loki chuckled and stole away to think up a means of making Skadi laugh.

Finally, the gods agreed that Skadi should choose one of them for her husband; but in order that all might have a fair chance of missing this honor which no one coveted, she was to choose in a curious way. All the Æsir were to stand in a row behind the curtain which was drawn across the end of the hall, so that only their feet were seen by Skadi; and by their feet alone Skadi was to select him who was to be her husband.

Now Skadi was very ready to agree to this, for she said to herself, "Surely, I shall know the feet of Balder, for they will be the most beautiful of any."

Amid nervous laughter at this new game, the Æsir ranged themselves in a row behind the purple curtain, with only their line of feet showing below the golden border. There were Father Odin, Thor the Thunderer, and Balder his brother; there was old Niörd the rich, with his fair son Frey; there were Týr the bold, Bragi the poet, blind Höd, and Vidar the silent; Vali and Ull the archers, Forseti the wise judge, and Heimdal the gold-toothed watchman. Loki alone, of all the Æsir, was not there; and Loki was the only one who did not shiver as Skadi walked up and down the hall looking at the row of feet.

Up and down, back and forth, went Skadi, looking carefully; and among all those sandaled feet there was one pair more white and fair and beautiful than the rest. "Surely, these are Balder's feet!" she thought, while her heart thumped with eagerness under her silver corselet. "Oh, if I guess aright, dear Balder will be my husband!"

She paused confidently before the handsomest pair of

feet, and, pointing to them with her spear, she cried, "I choose here! Few blemishes are to be found in Balder the beautiful."

A shout of laughter arose behind the curtain, and forth slunk—not young Balder, but old Niörd the rich, king of the ocean wind, the father of those fair twins, Frey and Freia. Skadi had chosen the handsome feet of old Niörd, and thenceforth he must be her husband.

Niörd was little pleased; but Skadi was heart-broken. Her face grew longer and sadder than before when he stepped up and took her hand sulkily, saying, "Well, I am to be your husband, then, and all my riches stored in Noatûn, the home of ships, are to be yours. You would have chosen Balder, and I wish that this luck had been his! However, it cannot be helped now."

"Nay," answered Skadi, frowning, "the bargain is not yet complete. No one of you has made me laugh. I am so sad now, that it will be a merry jest indeed which can wring laughter from my heavy heart." She sighed, looking at Balder. But Balder loved only Nanna in all the world.

Just then, out came Loki, riding on one of Thor's goat steeds; and the red-bearded fellow cut up such ridiculous capers with the gray-bearded goat that soon not only Skadi, but all the Æsir and Niörd himself were holding their sides with laughter.

"Fairly won, fairly won!" cried Skadi, wiping the tears from her eyes. "I am beaten. I shall not forget that it is Loki to whom I owe this last joke. Some day I shall be quits with you, red joker!" And this threat she carried out in the end, on the day of Loki's punishment.

Skadi was married to old Niörd, both unwilling; and they went to live among the mountains in Skadi's home, which had once been Thiasse's palace, where he had shut Idun in a prison cell. As you can imagine, Niörd and Skadi did not live happily ever after, like the good prince and princess in the story-book. For, in the first place, Skadi was a giantess; and there are few folk, I fancy, who could

live happily with a giantess. In the second place, she did
not love Niörd, nor did he love Skadi, and neither forgot
that Skadi's choosing had been sorrow to them both. But
the third reason was the most important of all; and this
was because Skadi and Niörd could not agree upon the
place which should be their home. For Niörd did not like
the mountain palace of Skadi's people,—the place where
roaring winds rushed down upon the sea and its ships.
The sea with its ships was his friend, and he wanted to
dwell in Noatûn, where he had greater wealth than any
one else in the world,—where he could rule the fresh sea-
wind and tame the wild ocean, granting the prayers of
fisher-folk and the seafarers, who loved his name.

Finally, they agreed to dwell first in one place, then in
the other, so that each might be happy in turn. For nine
days they tarried in Thrymheim, and then they spent
three in Noatûn. But even this arrangement could not
bring peace. One day they had a terrible quarrel. It was
just after they had come down from Skadi's mountain
home for their three days in Niörd's sea palace, and he
was so glad to be back that he cried,—

"Ah, how I hate your hills! How long the nine nights
seemed, with the wolves howling until dawn among the
dark mountains of Giant Land! What a discord compared
to the songs of the swans who sail upon my dear, dear
ocean!" Thus rudely he taunted his wife; but Skadi
answered him with spirit.

"And I—I cannot sleep by your rolling sea-waves, where
the birds are ever calling, calling, as they come from the
woods on the shore. Each morning the sea-gull's scream
wakes me at some unseemly hour. I will not stay here even
for three nights! I will not stay!"

"And I will have no more of your windy mountain-tops,"
roared Niörd, beside himself with rage. "Go, if you wish!
Go back to Thrymheim! I shall not follow you, be sure!"

So Skadi went back to her mountains alone, and dwelt
in the empty house of Thiasse, her father. She became a

mighty huntress, swift on the skees and ice-runners which she strapped to her feet. Day after day she skimmed over the snow-crusted mountains, bow in hand, to hunt the wild beasts which roamed there. "Skee-goddess," she was called; and never again did she come to Asgard halls. Quite alone in the cold country, she hunted hardily, keeping ever in her heart the image of Balder the beautiful, whom she loved, but whom she had lost forever by her unlucky choice.

The Dwarf's Gifts

Red Loki had been up to mischief again! Loki, who made quarrels and brought trouble wherever he went. He had a wicked heart, and he loved no one. He envied Father Odin his wisdom and his throne above the world. He envied Balder his beauty, and Týr his courage, and Thor his strength. He envied all the good Æsir who were happy; but he would not take the trouble to be good himself. So he was always unhappy, spiteful, and sour. And if anything went wrong in Asgard, the kingdom of the gods, one was almost sure to find Loki at the bottom of the trouble.

Now Thor, the strongest of all the gods, was very proud of his wife's beautiful hair, which fell in golden waves to her feet, and covered her like a veil. He loved it better than anything, except Sif herself. One day, while Thor was away from home, Loki stole into Thrudheim, the realm of clouds, and cut off all Sif's golden hair, till her head was as round and fuzzy as a yellow dandelion. Fancy how angry Thor was when he came rattling home that night in his thunder-chariot and found Sif so ugly to look at! He stamped up and down till the five hundred and forty floors of his cloud palace shook like an earthquake, and lightning flashed from his blue eyes. The people down in the world below cried: "Dear, dear! What a terrible thunderstorm! Thor must be very angry about something. Loki has been up to mischief, it is likely." You see, they also knew Loki and his tricks.

At last Thor calmed himself a little. "Sif, my love," he

said, "you shall be beautiful again. Red Loki shall make you so, since his was the unmaking. The villain! He shall pay for this!"

Then, without more ado, off set Thor to find red Loki. He went in his thunder-chariot, drawn by two goats, and the clouds rumbled and the lightning flashed wherever he went; for Thor was the mighty god of thunder. At last he came upon the sly rascal, who was trying to hide. Big Thor seized him by the throat.

"You scoundrel!" he cried, "I will break every bone in your body if you do not put back Sif's beautiful hair upon her head."

"Ow—ow! You hurt me!" howled Loki. "Take off your big hand, Thor. What is done, is done. I cannot put back Sif's hair. You know that very well."

"Then you must get her another head of hair," growled Thor. "That you can do. You must find for her hair of real gold, and it must grow upon her head as if it were her own. Do this, or you shall die."

"Where shall I get this famous hair?" whined Loki, though he knew well enough.

"Get it of the black elves," said Thor; "they are cunning jewelers, and they are your friends. Go, Loki, and go quickly, for I long to see Sif as beautiful as ever."

Then Loki of the burning beard slunk away to the hills where, far under ground, the dwarfs have their furnaces and their work-shops. Among great heaps of gold and silver and shining jewels, which they have dug up out of the earth, the little crooked men in brown blink and chatter and scold one another; for they are ugly fellows—the dwarfs. *Tink-tank! tink-tank!* go their little hammers all day long and all night long, while they make wonderful things such as no man has ever seen, though you shall hear about them.

They had no trouble to make a head of hair for Sif. It was for them a simple matter, indeed. The dwarfs work fast for such a customer as Loki, and in a little while the golden wires were beaten out, and drawn out, made smooth and soft and curly, and braided into a thick golden braid. But when Loki came away, he carried with him also two other treasures which the clever dwarfs had made. One was a golden spear, and the other was a ship.

Now these do not sound so very wonderful. But wait until you hear! The spear, which was named Gungnir, was bewitched, so that it made no difference if the person who held it was clumsy and careless. For it had this amazing quality, that no matter how badly it was aimed, or how unskillfully it was thrown, it was sure to go straight to the mark—which is a very obliging and convenient thing in one's weapon, as you will readily see.

And Skidbladnir—this was the harsh name of the ship— was even more wonderful. It could be taken to pieces and folded up so small that it would go into one's pocket. But when it was unfolded and put together, it would hold all the gods of Asgard for a sea-journey. Besides all this, when the sails were set, the ship was sure always to have a fair wind, which would make it skim along like a great bird, which was the best part of the charm, as any sailor will tell you.

Now Loki felt very proud of these three treasures, and left the hill cave stretching his neck and strutting like a great red turkey cock. Outside the gate, however, he met Brock, the black dwarf, who was the brother of Sindri, the best workman in all the underworld.

"Hello! what have you there?" asked Brock of the big head, pointing at the bundles which Loki was carrying.

"The three finest gifts in the world," boasted Loki, hugging his treasures tight.

"Pooh!" said Brock, "I don't believe it. Did my brother Sindri make them?"

"No," answered Loki; "they were made by the black elves, the sons of Ivaldi. And they are the most precious gifts that ever were seen."

"Pooh!" again puffed Brock, wagging his long beard

crossly. "Nonsense! Whatever they be, my brother Sindri can make three other gifts more precious; that I know."

"Can he, though?" laughed Loki. "I will give him my head if he can."

"Done!" shouted the dwarf. "Let me see your famous gifts." So Loki showed him the three wonders: the gold hair for Sif, the spear, and the ship. But again the dwarf said: "Pooh! These are nothing. I will show you what the master-smith can do, and you shall lose your bragging red head, my Loki."

Now Loki began to be a little uneasy. He followed Brock back to the smithy in the mountain, where they found Sindri at his forge. Oh, yes! He could beat the poor gifts of which Loki was so proud. But he would not tell what his own three gifts were to be.

First Sindri took a pig's skin and laid it on the fire. Then he went away for a little time; but he set Brock at the bellows and bade him blow—blow—blow the fire until Sindri should return. Now when Sindri was gone, Loki also stole away; for, as usual, he was up to mischief. He had the power of changing his shape and of becoming any creature he chose, which was often very convenient. Thus he turned himself into a huge biting fly. Then he flew back into the smithy where Brock was blow—blow—blowing. Loki buzzed about the dwarf's head, and finally lighted on his hand and stung him, hoping to make him let go the bellows. But no! Brock only cried out, "Oh-ee!" and kept on blowing for dear life. Now soon back came Sindri to the forge and took the pigskin from the fire. Wonder of wonders! It had turned into a hog with golden bristles; a live hog that shone like the sun. Brock was not satisfied, however.

"Well! I don't think much of that," he grumbled.

"Wait a little," said Sindri mysteriously. "Wait and see." Then he went on to make the second gift.

This time he put a lump of gold into the fire. And when he went away, as before, he bade Brock stand at the bellows to blow—blow—blow without stopping. Again, as before, in buzzed Loki the gadfly as soon as the master-smith had gone out. This time he settled on Brock's swarthy neck, and stung him so sorely that the blood came and the dwarf roared till the mountain trembled. Still Brock did not let go the handle of the bellows, but blew and howled—blew and howled with pain till Sindri returned. And this time the dwarf took from the fire a fine gold ring, round as roundness.

"Um! I don't think so much of that," said Brock, again disappointed, for he had expected some wonderful jewel. But Sindri wagged his head wisely.

"Wait a little," he said. "We shall see what we shall see." He heaved a great lump of iron into the fire to make the third gift. But this time when he went away, leaving Brock at the bellows, he charged him to blow—blow—blow without a minute's rest, or everything would be spoiled. For this was to be the best gift of all.

Brock planted himself wide-legged at the forge and blew—blew—blew. But for the third time Loki, winged as a fly, came buzzing into the smithy. This time he fastened viciously below Brock's bushy eyebrow, and stung him so cruelly that the blood trickled down, a red river, into his eyes and the poor dwarf was blinded. With a howl Brock raised his hand to wipe away the blood, and of course in that minute the bellows stood still. Then Loki buzzed away with a sound that seemed like a mocking laugh. At the same moment in rushed Sindri, panting with fright, for he had heard that sound and guessed what it meant.

"What have you done?" he cried. "You have let the bellows rest! You have spoiled everything!"

"Only a little moment, but one little moment," pleaded Brock, in a panic. "It has done no harm, has it?"

Sindri leaned anxiously over the fire, and out of the flames he drew the third gift—an enormous hammer.

"Oh!" said Brock, much disappointed, "only an old iron hammer! I don't think anything of *that*. Look how short the handle is, too."

"That is your fault, brother," returned the smith crossly. "If you had not let the bellows stand still, the handle

The third gift—an enormous hammer.
See page 50.

would have been long enough. Yet as it is—we shall see, we shall see. I think it will at least win for you red Loki's head. Take the three gifts, brother, such as they are, and bear them to Asgard. Let all the gods be judges between you and Loki, which gifts are best, his or yours. But stay— I may as well tell you the secrets of your three treasures, or you will not know how to make them work. Your toy that is not wound up is of no use at all." Which is very true, as we all know. Then he bent over and whispered in Brock's ear. And what he said pleased Brock so much that he jumped straight up into the air and capered like one of Thor's goats.

"What a clever brother you are, to be sure!" he cried.

At that moment Loki, who had ceased to be a gadfly, came in grinning, with his three gifts. "Well, are you ready?" he asked. Then he caught sight of the three gifts which Brock was putting into his sack.

"Ho! A pig, a ring, and a stub-handled hammer!" he shouted. "Is that all you have? Fine gifts, indeed! I was really growing uneasy, but now I see that my head is safe. Let us start for Asgard immediately, where I promise you that I with my three treasures shall be thrice more welcome than you with your stupid pig, your ugly ring, and your half-made hammer."

So together they climbed to Asgard, and there they found the Æsir sitting in the great judgment hall on Ida Plain. There was Father Odin on his high throne, with his two ravens at his head and his two wolves at his feet. There was Queen Frigg by his side; and about them were Balder the beautiful, Frey and Freia, the fair brother and sister; the mighty Thor, with Sif his crop-haired wife, and all the rest of the great Æsir who lived in the upper world above the homes of men.

"Brother Æsir," said Loki, bowing politely, for he was a smooth rascal, "we have come each with three gifts, the dwarf and I; and you shall judge which be the most worthy of praise. But if I lose,—I, your brother,—I lose my head to this crooked little dwarf." So he spoke, hoping to put the Æsir on his side from the first. For his head was a very handsome one, and the dwarf was indeed an ill-looking fellow. The gods, however, nodded gravely, and bade the two show what their gifts might be.

Then Loki stepped forward to the foot of Odin's throne. And first he pulled from his great wallet the spear Gungnir, which could not miss aim. This he gave to Odin, the all-wise. And Odin was vastly pleased, as you may imagine, to find himself thenceforth an unequaled marksman. So he smiled upon Loki kindly and said: "Well done, brother."

Next Loki took out the promised hair for Sif, which he handed Thor with a grimace. Now when the golden locks were set upon her head, they grew there like real hair, long and soft and curling—but still real gold. So that Sif was more beautiful than ever before, and more precious, too. You can fancy how pleased Thor was with Loki's gift. He kissed lovely Sif before all the gods and goddesses, and vowed that he forgave Loki for the mischief which he had done in the first place, since he had so nobly made reparation.

Then Loki took out the third gift, all folded up like a paper boat; and it was the ship Skidbladnir,—I am sorry they did not give it a prettier name. This he presented to Frey the peaceful. And you can guess whether or not Frey's blue eyes laughed with pleasure at such a gift.

Now when Loki stepped back, all the Æsir clapped their hands and vowed that he had done wondrous well.

"You will have to show us fine things, you dwarf," quoth Father Odin, "to better the gifts of red Loki. Come, what have you in the sack you bear upon your shoulders?"

Then the crooked little Brock hobbled forward, bent almost double under the great load which he carried. "I have what I have," he said.

First, out he pulled the ring Draupnir, round as roundness and shining of gold. This the dwarf gave to Odin, and though it seemed but little, yet it was much. For every ninth night out of this ring, he said, would drop eight other rings of gold, as large and as fair. Then Odin clapped his hands and cried: "Oh, wondrous gift! I like it even better than the magic spear which Loki gave." And all the other Æsir agreed with him.

Then out of the sack came grunting Goldbristle, the hog, all of gold. Brock gave him to Frey, to match the magic ship of Loki. This Goldbristle was so marvelously forged that he could run more swiftly than any horse, on air or water. Moreover, he was a living lantern. For on the darkest night he bristled with light like a million-pointed star, so that one riding on his back would light the air and the sea like a firefly, wherever he went. This idea pleased Frey mightily, for he was the merriest of the gods, and he laughed aloud.

"'Tis a wondrous fine gift," he said. "I like old Goldbristle even better than the compressible boat. For on this lusty steed I can ride about the world when I am tending the crops and the cattle of men and scattering the rain upon them. Master dwarf, I give my vote to you." And all the other Æsir agreed with him.

Then out of the sack Brock drew the third gift. It was the short-handled hammer named Miölnir. And this was the gift which Sindri had made for Thor, the mightiest of the gods; and it was the best gift of all. For with it Thor could burst the hardest metal and shatter the thickest mountain, and nothing could withstand its power. But it never could hurt Thor himself; and no matter how far or how hard it was thrown, it would always fly back into Thor's own hand. Last of all, whenever he so wished, the great hammer would become so small that he could put it in his pocket, quite out of sight. But Brock was sorry that the handle was so short—all owing to his fault, because he had let the bellows rest for that one moment.

When Thor had this gift in his hand, he jumped up with a shout of joy. " 'Tis a wondrous fine gift," he cried, "with short handle or with long. And I prize it even more than I prize the golden hair of Sif which Loki gave. For with it I shall fight our enemies, the Frost Giants and the mischievous Trolls and the other monsters—Loki's friends. And all the Æsir will be glad of my gift when they see what deeds I shall do therewith. Now, if I may have my say, I judge that the three gifts made by Sindri the dwarf are the most precious that may be. So Brock has gained the prize of Loki's red head,—a sorry recompense indeed for gifts so masterly." Then Thor sat down. And all the other Æsir shouted that he had spoken well, and that they agreed with him.

So Loki was like to lose his head. He offered to pay instead a huge price, if Brock would let him go. But Brock refused. "The red head of Loki for my gift," he insisted, and the gods nodded that it must be so, since he had earned his wish.

But when Loki saw that the count was all against him, his eyes grew crafty. "Well, take me, then—if you can!" he shouted. And off he shot like an arrow from a bow. For Loki had on magic shoes, with which he could run over sea or land or sky; and the dwarf could never catch him in the world. Then Brock was furious. He stood stamping and chattering, tearing his long beard with rage.

"I am cheated!" he cried. "I have won—but I have lost." Then he turned to Thor, who was playing with his hammer, bursting a mountain or two and splitting a tree here and there. "Mighty Thor," begged the dwarf, "catch me the fellow who has broken his word. I have given you the best gift,—your wonderful hammer. Catch me, then, the boasting red head which I have fairly bought."

Then Thor stopped his game and set out in pursuit of Loki, for he was ever on the side of fairness. No one, however fleet, can escape when Thor follows, for his is the swiftness of a lightning flash. So he soon brought Loki back to Ida Plain, and gave him up a prisoner to the dwarf.

"I have you now, boaster," said Brock fiercely, "and I will cut off your red head in the twinkling of an eye." But just as he was about to do as he said, Loki had another sly idea.

"Hold, sirrah dwarf," he said. "It is true that you have

won my head, but not the neck, not an inch of the neck."
And all the gods agreed that this was so. Then Brock was
puzzled indeed, for how could he cut off Loki's head without an inch of the neck, too? But this he must not do, or
he knew the just Æsir would punish him with death. So he
was forced to be content with stopping Loki's boasting in
another way. He would sew up the bragging lips.

He brought a stout, strong thread and an awl to bore
the holes. And in a twinkling he had stitched up the lips of
the sly one, firm and fast. So for a time, at least, he put an
end to Loki's boasting and his taunts and his lies.

It is a pity that those mischief-making lips were not fastened up forever; for that would have saved much of the
trouble and sorrow which came after. But at last, after a
long time, Loki got his lips free, and they made great sorrow in Asgard for the gods and on earth for men, as you
shall hear.

Now this is the end of the tale which tells of the dwarf's
gifts, and especially of Thor's hammer, which was afterwards to be of such service to him and such bane to the
enemies of the Æsir. And that also you shall hear before
all is done.

Loki's Children

Red Loki, the wickedest of all the Æsir, had done something of which he was very much ashamed. He had married a giantess, the ugliest, fiercest, most dreadful giantess that ever lived; and of course he wanted no one to find out what he had done, for he knew that Father Odin would be indignant with him for having wedded one of the enemies of the Æsir, and that none of his brothers would be grateful to him for giving them a sister-in-law so hideous.

But at last All-Father found out the secret that Loki had been hiding for years. Worst of all, he found that Loki and the giantess had three ugly children hidden away in the dark places of the earth,—three children of whom Loki was even more ashamed than of their mother, though he loved them too. For two of them were the most terrible monsters which time had ever seen. Hela his daughter was the least ugly of the three, though one could scarcely call her attractive. She was half black and half white, which must have looked very strange; and she was not easily mistaken by any one who chanced to see her, you can well understand. She was fierce and grim to see, and the very sight of her caused terror and death to him who gazed upon her.

But the other two! One was an enormous wolf, with long fierce teeth and flashing red eyes. And the other was a scaly, slimy, horrible serpent, huger than any serpent that ever lived, and a hundred times more ferocious. Can you wonder that Loki was ashamed of such children as these? The wonder is, how he could find anything about them to love. But Loki's heart loved evil in secret, and it was the evil in these three children of his which made them so ugly.

Now when Odin discovered that three such monsters had been living in the world without his knowledge, he was both angry and anxious, for he knew that these children of mischievous Loki and his wicked giantess-wife were dangerous to the peace of Asgard. He consulted the Norns, the three wise maidens who lived beside the Urdar-well, and who could see into the future to tell what things were to happen in coming years. And they bade him beware of Loki's children; they told him that the three monsters would bring great sorrow upon Asgard, for the giantess their mother would teach them all her hatred of Odin's race, while they would have their father's sly wisdom to help them in all mischief. So Odin knew that his fears had warned him truly. Something must be done to prevent the dangers which threatened Asgard. Something must be done to keep the three out of mischief.

Father Odin sent for all the gods, and bade them go forth over the world, find the children of Loki in the secret places where they were hidden, and bring them to him. Then the Æsir mounted their horses and set out on their difficult errand. They scoured Asgard, Midgard the world of men, Utgard and Jotunheim where the giants lived. And at last they found the three horrible creatures hiding in their mother's cave. They dragged them forth and took them up to Asgard, before Odin's high throne.

Now All-Father had been considering what should be done with the three monsters, and when they came, his mind was made up. Hela, the daughter, was less evil than the other two, but her face was dark and gloomy, and she brought death to those who looked upon her. She must be prisoned out of sight in some far place, where her sad eyes could not look sorrow into men's lives and death into their hearts. So he sent her down, down into the dark, cold land of Niflheim, which lay below one root of the great tree Yggdrasil. Here she must live forever and ever. And, because she was not wholly bad, Odin made her queen of that land, and for her subjects she was to have all the folk who died upon the earth,—except the heroes who perished in battle; for these the Valkyries carried straight to Valhalla in Asgard. But all who died of sickness or of old age, all who met their deaths through accident or men's cruelty, were sent to Queen Hela, who gave them lodgings in her gloomy palace. Vast was her kingdom, huge as nine worlds, and it was surrounded by a high wall, so that no one who had once gone thither could ever return. And here thenceforth Loki's daughter reigned among the shadows, herself half shadow and half light, half good and half bad.

But the Midgard serpent was a more dangerous beast even than Death. Odin frowned when he looked upon this monster writhing before his throne. He seized the scaly length in his mighty arms and hurled it forth over the wall of Asgard. Down, down went the great serpent, twisting and twirling as he fell, while all the sky was black with the smoke from his nostrils, and the sound of his hissing made every creature tremble. Down, down he fell with a great splash into the deep ocean which surrounded the world. There he lay writhing and squirming, growing always larger and larger, until he was so huge that he stretched like a ring about the whole earth, with his tail in his mouth, and his wicked eyes glaring up through the water towards Asgard which he hated. Sometimes he heaved himself up, great body and all, trying to escape from the ocean which was his prison. At those times there were great waves in the sea, snow and stormy winds and rain upon the earth, and every one would be filled with fear lest he escape and bring horrors to pass. But he was never able to drag out his whole hideous length. For the evil in him had grown with his growth; and a weight of evil is the heaviest of all things to lift.

The third monster was the Fenris wolf, and this was the most dreadful of the three. He was so terrible that at first Father Odin decided not to let him out of his sight. He lived in Asgard then, among the Æsir. Only Týr the brave had courage enough to give him food. Day by day he grew huger and huger, fiercer and fiercer, and finally, when All-Father saw how mighty he had become, and how he bid fair to bring destruction upon all Asgard if he were allowed to prowl and growl about as he saw fit, Odin resolved to have the beast chained up. The Æsir then went to their smithies and forged a long, strong chain which they thought no living creature could break. They took it to the wolf to try its strength, and he, looking side-wise, chuckled to himself and let them do what they would with him. But as soon as he stretched himself, the chain burst into a thousand pieces, as if it were made of twine. Then the Æsir hurried away and made another chain, far, far stronger than the first.

"If you can break this, O Fenrir," they said, "you will be famous indeed."

Again the wolf blinked at his chain; again he chuckled and let them fasten him without a struggle, for he knew that his own strength had been increased since he broke the other; but as soon as the chain was fastened, he shook his great shoulders, kicked his mighty legs, and—snap!—the links of the chain went whirling far and wide, and once more the fierce beast was free.

Then the Æsir were alarmed for fear that they would never be able to make a chain mighty enough to hold the wolf, who was growing stronger every minute; but they sent Skirnir, Frey's trusty messenger, to the land of the dwarfs for help. "Make us a chain," was the message he bore from the Æsir,—"make us a chain stronger than any chain that was ever forged; for the Fenris wolf must be captured and bound, or all the world must pay the penalty."

The dwarfs were the finest workmen in the world, as the Æsir knew; for it was they who made Thor's hammer, and Odin's spear, and Balder's famous ship, besides many other wondrous things that you remember. So when Skirnir gave them the message, they set to work with their little hammers and anvils, and before long they had welded a wonderful chain, such as no man had ever before seen. Strange things went to the making of it,—the sound of a cat's footsteps, the roots of a mountain, a bear's sinews, a fish's breath, and other magic materials that only the dwarfs knew how to put together; and the result was a chain as soft and twistable as a silken cord, but stronger than an iron cable. With this chain Skirnir galloped back to Asgard, and with it the gods were sure of chaining Fenrir; but they meant to go about the business slyly, so that the wolf should not suspect the danger which was so near.

"Ho, Fenrir!" they cried. "Here is a new chain for you. Do you think you can snap this as easily as you did the last? We warn you that it is stronger than it looks." They handed it about from one to another, each trying to break the links, but in vain. The wolf watched them disdainfully.

"Pooh! There is little honor in breaking a thread so slender!" he said. "I know that I could snap it with one bite of my big teeth. But there may be some trick about it; I will not let it bind my feet,—not I."

"Oho!" cried the Æsir. "He is afraid! He fears that we shall bind him in cords that he cannot loose. But see how slender the chain is. Surely, if you could burst the chain of iron, O Fenrir, you could break this far more easily." Still the wolf shook his head, and refused to let them fasten him, suspecting some trick. "But even if you find that you cannot break our chain," they said, "you need not be afraid. We shall set you free again."

"Set me free!" growled the wolf. "Yes, you will set me free at the end of the world,—not before! I know your ways, O Æsir; and if you are able to bind me so fast that I cannot free myself, I shall wait long to have the chain made loose. But no one shall call me coward. If one of you will place his hand in my mouth and hold it there while the others bind me, I will let the chain be fastened."

The gods looked at one another, their mouths drooping. Who would do this thing and bear the fury of the angry wolf when he should find himself tricked and captured? Yet this was their only chance to bind the monster and protect Asgard from danger. At last bold Týr stepped forward, the bravest of all the Æsir. "Open your mouth, Fenrir," he cried, with a laugh. "I will pledge my hand to the trial."

Then the wolf yawned his great jaws, and Týr thrust in his good right hand, knowing full well that he was to lose it in the game. The Æsir stepped up with the dwarfs' magic chain, and Fenrir let them fasten it about his feet. But when the bonds were drawn tight, he began to struggle; and the more he tugged, the tighter drew the chain, so that he soon saw himself to be entrapped. Then how he writhed and kicked, howled and growled, in his terrible rage! How the heavens trembled and the earth shook below! The Æsir set up a laugh to see him so helpless—all except Týr; for at the first sound of laughter the wolf shut his great mouth with a click, and poor brave Týr had lost the right hand which had done so many heroic deeds in battle, and which would never again wave sword before the warriors whom he loved and would help to win the victory. But great was the honor which he won that day, for without his generous deed the Fenris wolf could never have been captured.

And now the monster was safely secured by the strong chain which the dwarfs had made, and all his struggles to be free were in vain, for they only bound the silken rope all the tighter. The Æsir took one end of the chain and fastened it through a big rock which they planted far down in the earth, as far as they could drive it with a huge hammer of stone. Into the wolf's great mouth they thrust a sword crosswise, so that the hilt pierced his lower jaw while the point stuck through the upper one; and there in the heart of the world he lay howling and growling, but quite unable to move. Only the foam which dripped from his angry jaws trickled away and over the earth until it formed a mighty river; from his wicked mouth also came smoke and fire, and the sound of his horrible growls. And when men hear this and see this they run away as fast as they can, for they know that danger still lurks near where the Fenris wolf lies chained in the depths of the earth; and here he will lie until Ragnarök,—until the end of all things.

The Quest of the Hammer

One morning Thor the Thunderer awoke with a yawn, and stretching out his knotted arm, felt for his precious hammer, which he kept always under his pillow of clouds. But he started up with a roar of rage, so that all the palace trembled. The hammer was gone!

Now this was a very serious matter, for Thor was the protector of Asgard, and Miölnir, the magic hammer which the dwarf had made, was his mighty weapon, of which the enemies of the Æsir stood so much in dread that they dared not venture near. But if they should learn that Miölnir was gone, who could tell what danger might not threaten the palaces of heaven?

Thor darted his flashing eye into every corner of Cloud Land in search of the hammer. He called his fair wife, Sif of the golden hair, to aid in the search, and his two lovely daughters, Thrude and Lora. They hunted and they hunted; they turned Thrudheim upside down, and set the clouds to rolling wonderfully, as they peeped and pried behind and around and under each billowy mass. But Miölnir was not to be found. Certainly, some one had stolen it.

Thor's yellow beard quivered with rage, and his hair bristled on end like the golden rays of a star, while all his household trembled.

"It is Loki again!" he cried. "I am sure Loki is at the bottom of this mischief!" For since the time when Thor had captured Loki for the dwarf Brock and had given him over to have his bragging lips sewed up, Loki had looked at him with evil eyes; and Thor knew that the red rascal hated him most of all the gods.

But this time Thor was mistaken. It was not Loki who had stolen the hammer,—he was too great a coward for that. And though he meant, before the end, to be revenged upon Thor, he was waiting until a safe chance should come, when Thor himself might stumble into danger, and Loki need only to help the evil by a malicious word or two; and this chance came later, as you shall hear in another tale.

Meanwhile Loki was on his best behavior, trying to appear very kind and obliging; so when Thor came rumbling and roaring up to him, demanding, "What have you done with my hammer, you thief?" Loki looked surprised, but did not lose his temper nor answer rudely.

"Have you indeed missed your hammer, brother Thor?" he said, mumbling, for his mouth was still sore where Brock had sewed the stitches. "That is a pity; for if the giants hear of this, they will be coming to try their might against Asgard."

"Hush!" muttered Thor, grasping him by the shoulder with his iron fingers. "That is what I fear. But look you, Loki: I suspect your hand in the mischief. Come, confess."

Then Loki protested that he had nothing to do with so wicked a deed. "But," he added wheedlingly, "I think I can guess the thief; and because I love you, Thor, I will help you to find him."

"Humph!" growled Thor. "Much love you bear to me! However, you are a wise rascal, the nimblest wit of all the Æsir, and it is better to have you on my side than on the other, when giants are in the game. Tell me, then: who has robbed the Thunder-Lord of his bolt of power?"

Loki drew near and whispered in Thor's ear. "Look, how the storms rage and the winds howl in the world below! Some one is wielding your thunder-hammer all unskillfully. Can you not guess the thief? Who but Thrym, the mighty giant who has ever been your enemy and your imitator, and whose fingers have long itched to grasp the short handle of mighty Miölnir, that the world may name him Thunder-Lord instead of you. But look! What a tempest! The world will be shattered into fragments unless we soon get the hammer back."

Then Thor roared with rage. "I will seek this impudent Thrym!" he cried. "I will crush him into bits, and teach him to meddle with the weapon of the Æsir!"

"Softly, softly," said Loki, smiling maliciously. "He is a shrewd giant, and a mighty. Even you, great Thor, cannot go to him and pluck the hammer from his hand as one would slip the rattle from a baby's pink fist. Nay, you must use craft, Thor; and it is I who will teach you, if you will be patient."

Thor was a brave, blunt fellow, and he hated the ways of Loki, his lies and his deceit. He liked best the way of warriors,—the thundering charge, the flash of weapons, and the heavy blow; but without the hammer he could not fight the giants hand to hand. Loki's advice seemed wise, and he decided to leave the matter to the Red One.

Loki was now all eagerness, for he loved difficulties which would set his wit in play and bring other folk into danger. "Look, now," he said. "We must go to Freia and borrow her falcon dress. But you must ask; for she loves me so little that she would scarce listen to me."

So first they made their way to Folkvang, the house of maidens, where Freia dwelt, the loveliest of all in Asgard. She was fairer than fair, and sweeter than sweet, and the tears from her flower-eyes made the dew which blessed the earth-flowers night and morning. Of her Thor borrowed the magic dress of feathers in which Freia was wont to clothe herself and flit like a great beautiful bird all about the world. She was willing enough to lend it to Thor when he told her that by its aid he hoped to win back the hammer which he had lost; for she well knew the danger threatening herself and all the Æsir until Miölnir should be found.

"Now will I fetch the hammer for you," said Loki. So he put on the falcon plumage, and, spreading his brown wings, flapped away up, up, over the world, down, down, across the great ocean which lies beyond all things that men know. And he came to the dark country where there was no sunshine nor spring, but it was always dreary winter; where mountains were piled up like blocks of ice, and where great caverns yawned hungrily in blackness. And this was Jotunheim, the land of the Frost Giants.

And lo! when Loki came thereto he found Thrym the Giant King sitting outside his palace cave, playing with his dogs and horses. The dogs were as big as elephants, and the horses were as big as houses, but Thrym himself was as huge as a mountain; and Loki trembled, but he tried to seem brave.

"Good-day, Loki," said Thrym, with the terrible voice of which he was so proud, for he fancied it was as loud as Thor's. "How fares it, feathered one, with your little brothers, the Æsir, in Asgard halls? And how dare you venture alone in this guise to Giant Land?"

"It is an ill day in Asgard," sighed Loki, keeping his eye warily upon the giant, "and a stormy one in the world of men. I heard the winds howling and the storms rushing on the earth as I passed by. Some mighty one has stolen the hammer of our Thor. Is it you, Thrym, greatest of all giants,—greater than Thor himself?"

This the crafty one said to flatter Thrym, for Loki well knew the weakness of those who love to be thought greater than they are.

Then Thrym bridled and swelled with pride, and tried to put on the majesty and awe of noble Thor; but he only succeeded in becoming an ugly, puffy monster.

"Well, yes," he admitted. "I have the hammer that belonged to your little Thor; and now how much of a lord is he?"

"Alack!" sighed Loki again, "weak enough he is without his magic weapon. But you, O Thrym,—surely your mightiness needs no such aid. Give me the hammer, that Asgard may no longer be shaken by Thor's grief for his precious toy."

But Thrym was not so easily to be flattered into parting with his stolen treasure. He grinned a dreadful grin, sev-

eral yards in width, which his teeth barred like jagged
boulders across the entrance to a mountain cavern.

"Miölnir the hammer is mine," he said, "and I am
Thunder-Lord, mightiest of the mighty. I have hidden it
where Thor can never find it, twelve leagues below the sea-
caves, where Queen Ran lives with her daughters, the white-
capped Waves. But listen, Loki. Go tell the Æsir that I will
give back Thor's hammer. I will give it back upon one condition,—that they send Freia the beautiful to be my wife."

"Freia the beautiful!" Loki had to stifle a laugh. Fancy
the Æsir giving their fairest flower to such an ugly fellow
as this! But he only said politely, "Ah, yes; you demand
our Freia in exchange for the little hammer? It is a costly
price, great Thrym. But I will be your friend in Asgard. If I
have my way, you shall soon see the fairest bride in all the
world knocking at your door. Farewell!"

So Loki whizzed back to Asgard on his falcon wings; and
as he went he chuckled to think of the evils which were
likely to happen because of his words with Thrym. First
he gave the message to Thor,—not sparing of Thrym's
insolence, to make Thor angry; and then he went to Freia
with the word for her,—not sparing of Thrym's ugliness,
to make her shudder. The spiteful fellow!

Now you can imagine the horror that was in Asgard as
the Æsir listened to Loki's words. "My hammer!" roared
Thor. "The villain confesses that he has stolen my hammer, and boasts that he is Thunder-Lord! Gr-r-r!"

"The ugly giant!" wailed Freia. "Must I be the bride of
that hideous old monster, and live in his gloomy mountain
prison all my life?"

"Yes; put on your bridal veil, sweet Freia," said Loki
maliciously, "and come with me to Jotunheim. Hang your
famous starry necklace about your neck, and don your
bravest robe; for in eight days there will be a wedding,
and Thor's hammer is to pay."

Then Freia fell to weeping. "I cannot go! I will not go!"
she cried. "I will not leave the home of gladness and
Father Odin's table to dwell in the land of horrors! Thor's

hammer is mighty, but mightier the love of the kind Æsir for their little Freia! Good Odin, dear brother Frey, speak for me! You will not make me go?"

The Æsir looked at her and thought how lonely and bare would Asgard be without her loveliness; for she was fairer than fair, and sweeter than sweet.

"She shall not go!" shouted Frey, putting his arms about his sister's neck.

"No, she shall not go!" cried all the Æsir with one voice.

"But my hammer," insisted Thor. "I must have Miölnir back again."

"And my word to Thrym," said Loki, "that must be made good."

"You are too generous with your words," said Father Odin sternly, for he knew his brother well. "Your word is not a gem of great price, for you have made it cheap."

Then spoke Heimdal, the sleepless watchman who sits on guard at the entrance to the rainbow bridge which leads to Asgard; and Heimdal was the wisest of the Æsir, for he could see into the future, and knew how things would come to pass. Through his golden teeth he spoke, for his teeth were all of gold.

"I have a plan," he said. "Let us dress Thor himself like a bride in Freia's robes, and send him to Jotunheim to talk with Thrym and to win back his hammer."

But at this word Thor grew very angry.

"What! dress me like a girl!" he roared. "I should never hear the last of it! The Æsir will mock me, and call me 'maiden'! The giants, and even the puny dwarfs, will have a lasting jest upon me! I will not go! I will fight! I will die, if need be! But dressed as a woman I will not go!"

But Loki answered him with sharp words, for this was a scheme after his own heart. "What, Thor!" he said. "Would you lose your hammer and keep Asgard in danger for so small a whim? Look, now: if you go not, Thrym with his giants will come in a mighty army and drive us from Asgard; then he will indeed make Freia his bride, and moreover he will have you for his slave under the power

"Ah, what a lovely maid it is!"
See page 70.

of his hammer. How like you this picture, brother of the thunder? Nay, Heimdal's plan is a good one, and I myself will help to carry it out."

Still Thor hesitated; but Freia came and laid her white hand on his arm, and looked up into his scowling face pleadingly.

"To save me, Thor," she begged. And Thor said he would go.

Then there was great sport among the Æsir, while they dressed Thor like a beautiful maiden. Brunhilde and her sisters, the nine Valkyrie, daughters of Odin, had the task in hand. How they laughed as they brushed and curled his yellow hair, and set upon it the wondrous headdress of silk and pearls! They let out seams, and they let down hems, and set on extra pieces, to make it larger, and so they hid his great limbs and knotted arms under Freia's fairest robe of scarlet; but beneath it all he would wear his shirt of mail and his belt of power that gave him double strength. Freia herself twisted about his neck her famous necklace of starry jewels, and Queen Frigg, his mother, hung at his girdle a jingling bunch of keys, such as was the custom for the bride to wear at Norse weddings. Last of all, that Thrym might not see Thor's fierce eyes and the yellow beard, that ill became a maiden, they threw over him a long veil of silver white which covered him to the feet. And there he stood, as stately and tall a bride as even a giant might wish to see; but on his hands he wore his iron gloves, and they ached for but one thing,—to grasp the handle of the stolen hammer.

"Ah, what a lovely maid it is!" chuckled Loki; "and how glad will Thrym be to see this Freia come! Bride Thor, I will go with you as your handmaiden, for I would fain see the fun."

"Come, then," said Thor sulkily, for he was ill pleased, and wore his maiden robes with no good grace. "It is fitting that you go; for I like not these lies and maskings, and I may spoil the mummery without you at my elbow."

There was loud laughter above the clouds when Thor,

all veiled and dainty seeming, drove away from Asgard to his wedding, with maid Loki by his side. Thor cracked his whip and chirruped fiercely to his twin goats with golden hoofs, for he wanted to escape the sounds of mirth that echoed from the rainbow bridge, where all the Æsir stood watching. Loki, sitting with his hands meekly folded like a girl, chuckled as he glanced up at Thor's angry face; but he said nothing, for he knew it was not good to joke too far with Thor, even when Miölnir was hidden twelve leagues below the sea in Ran's kingdom.

So off they dashed to Jotunheim, where Thrym was waiting and longing for his beautiful bride. Thor's goats thundered along above the sea and land and people far below, who looked up wondering as the noise rolled overhead. "Hear how the thunder rumbles!" they said. "Thor is on a long journey to-night." And a long journey it was, as the tired goats found before they reached the end.

Thrym heard the sound of their approach, for his ear was eager. "Hola!" he cried. "Some one is coming from Asgard,—only one of Odin's children could make a din so fearful. Hasten, men, and see if they are bringing Freia to be my wife."

Then the lookout giant stepped down from the top of his mountain, and said that a chariot was bringing two maidens to the door.

"Run, giants, run!" shouted Thrym, in a fever at this news. "My bride is coming! Put silken cushions on the benches for a great banquet, and make the house beautiful for the fairest maid in all space! Bring in all my golden-horned cows and my coal-black oxen, that she may see how rich I am, and heap all my gold and jewels about to dazzle her sweet eyes! She shall find me richest of the rich; and when I have her,—fairest of the fair,—there will be no treasure that I lack,—not one!"

The chariot stopped at the gate, and out stepped the tall bride, hidden from head to foot, and her handmaiden muffled to the chin. "How afraid of catching cold they must be!" whispered the giant ladies, who were peering over one another's shoulders to catch a glimpse of the bride, just as the crowd outside the awning does at a wedding nowadays.

Thrym had sent six splendid servants to escort the maidens: these were the Metal Kings, who served him as lord of them all. There was the Gold King, all in cloth of gold, with fringes of yellow bullion, most glittering to see; and there was the Silver King, almost as gorgeous in a suit of spangled white; and side by side bowed the dark Kings of Iron and Lead, the one mighty in black, the other sullen in blue; and after them were the Copper King, gleaming ruddy and brave, and the Tin King, strutting in his trimmings of gaudy tinsel which looked nearly as well as silver but were more economical. And this fine troop of lackey kings most politely led Thor and Loki into the palace, and gave them of the best, for they never suspected who these seeming maidens really were.

And when evening came there was a wonderful banquet to celebrate the wedding. On a golden throne sat Thrym, uglier than ever in his finery of purple and gold. Beside him was the bride, of whose face no one had yet caught even a glimpse; and at Thrym's other hand stood Loki, the waiting-maid, for he wanted to be near to mend the mistakes which Thor might make.

Now the dishes at the feast were served in a huge way, as befitted the table of giants: great beeves roasted whole, on platters as wide across as a ship's deck; plum-puddings as fat as feather-beds, with plums as big as footballs; and a wedding cake like a snow-capped haymow. The giants ate enormously. But to Thor, because they thought him a dainty maiden, they served small bits of everything on a tiny gold dish. Now Thor's long journey had made him very hungry, and through his veil he whispered to Loki, "I shall starve, Loki! I cannot fare on these nibbles. I must eat a goodly meal as I do at home." And forthwith he helped himself to such morsels as might satisfy his hunger for a little time. You should have seen the giants stare at the meal which the dainty bride devoured!

For first under the silver veil disappeared by pieces a whole roast ox. Then Thor made eight mouthfuls of eight pink salmon, a dish of which he was very fond. And next he looked about and reached for a platter of cakes and sweetmeats that was set aside at one end of the table for the lady guests, and the bride ate them all. You can fancy how the damsels drew down their mouths and looked at one another when they saw their dessert disappear; and they whispered about the table, "Alack! if our future mistress is to sup like this day by day, there will be poor cheer for the rest of us!" And to crown it all, Thor was thirsty, as well he might be; and one after another he raised to his lips and emptied three great barrels of mead, the foamy drink of the giants. Then indeed Thrym was amazed, for Thor's giant appetite had beaten that of the giants themselves.

"Never before saw I a bride so hungry!" he cried, "and never before one half so thirsty!"

But Loki, the waiting-maid, whispered to him softly, "The truth is, great Thrym, that my dear mistress was almost starved. For eight days Freia has eaten nothing at all, so eager was she for Jotunheim."

Then Thrym was delighted, you may be sure. He forgave his hungry bride, and loved her with all his heart. He leaned forward to give her a kiss, raising a corner of her veil; but his hand dropped suddenly, and he started up in terror, for he had caught the angry flash of Thor's eye, which was glaring at him through the bridal veil. Thor was longing for his hammer.

"Why has Freia so sharp a look?" Thrym cried. "It pierces like lightning and burns like fire."

But again the sly waiting-maid whispered timidly, "Oh, Thrym, be not amazed! The truth is, my poor mistress's eyes are red with wakefulness and bright with longing. For eight nights Freia has not known a wink of sleep, so eager was she for Jotunheim."

Then again Thrym was doubly delighted, and he longed to call her his very own dear wife. "Bring in the wedding

gift!" he cried. "Bring in Thor's hammer, Miölnir, and give
it to Freia, as I promised; for when I have kept my word
she will be mine,—all mine!"

Then Thor's big heart laughed under his woman's
dress, and his fierce eyes swept eagerly down the hall to
meet the servant who was bringing in the hammer on a
velvet cushion. Thor's fingers could hardly wait to clutch
the stubby handle which they knew so well; but he sat
quite still on the throne beside ugly old Thrym, with his
hands meekly folded and his head bowed like a bashful
bride.

The giant servant drew nearer, nearer, puffing and blowing, strong though he was, beneath the mighty weight. He
was about to lay it at Thor's feet (for he thought it so
heavy that no maiden could lift it or hold it in her lap),
when suddenly Thor's heart swelled, and he gave a most
unmaidenly shout of rage and triumph. With one swoop
he grasped the hammer in his iron fingers; with the other
arm he tore off the veil that hid his terrible face, and tram-
pled it under foot; then he turned to the frightened king,
who cowered beside him on the throne.

"Thief!" he cried. "Freia sends you *this* as a wedding
gift!" And he whirled the hammer about his head, then
hurled it once, twice, thrice, as it rebounded to his hand;
and in the first stroke, as of lightning, Thrym rolled dead
from his throne; in the second stroke perished the whole
giant household,—these ugly enemies of the Æsir; and in
the third stroke the palace itself tumbled together and fell
to the ground like a toppling play-house of blocks.

But Loki and Thor stood safely among the ruins,
dressed in their tattered maiden robes, a quaint and curious sight; and Loki, full of mischief now as ever, burst out
laughing.

"Oh, Thor! if you could see"— he began; but Thor held
up his hammer and shook it gently as he said,—

"Look now, Loki: it was an excellent joke, and so far you
have done well,—after your crafty fashion, which likes me
not. But now I have my hammer again, and the joke is

done. From you, nor from another, I brook no laughter at my expense. Henceforth we will have no mention of this masquerade, nor of these rags which now I throw away. Do you hear, red laugher?"

And Loki heard, with a look of hate, and stifled his laughter as best he could; for it is not good to laugh at him who holds the hammer.

Not once after that was there mention in Asgard of the time when Thor dressed him as a girl and won his bridal gift from Thrym the giant.

But Miölnir was safe once more in Asgard, and you and I know how it came there; so some one must have told. I wonder if red Loki whispered the tale to some outsider, after all? Perhaps it may be so, for now he knew how best to make Thor angry; and from that day when Thor forbade his laughing, Loki hated him with the mean little hatred of a mean little soul.

The Giantess Who Would Not

Of all the Æsir who sat in the twelve seats about Father Odin's wonder-throne none was so dear to the people of Midgard, the world of men, as Frey. For Frey, the twin brother of Freia the fair, was the god who sent sunshine and rain upon the earth that men's crops might grow and ripen, and the fruits become sweet and mellow. He gave men cattle, and showed them how to till the fields; and it was he who spread peace and prosperity over the world. For he was lord of the Light-Elves, the spirits of the upper air, who were more beautiful than the sun. And these were his servants whom he sent to answer the prayers of the men who loved him. Frey was more beautiful, too, than any of the Æsir except young Balder. This was another reason why he was so beloved by all. But there came a time when Frey found some one who would not love him; and that was a new experience for him, a punishment for the only wrong he ever committed.

You remember that Father Odin had a wonderful throne in the silver-roofed house, a throne whence he could see everything that was happening in all the world? Well, no one was allowed to sit upon this throne except All-Father himself, for he would not have the others spying into affairs which only the King of Asgard was wise enough to understand. But one day, when Odin was away from home, Frey had such a longing to climb up where he might gaze upon all the world which he loved, that he could not resist the temptation. He stole up to the great throne when no one was looking, and mounting the steps, seated himself upon All-Father's wonder-seat.

Oh, marvelous, grand, and beautiful! He looked off into the heavens, and there he saw all the Æsir busy about their daily work. He looked above, into the shining realm of clear air. And there he saw his messengers, the pretty little Light-Elves, flying about upon their errands of help for men. Some were carrying seeds for the farmers to plant. Some were watering the fields with their little water-pots, making the summer showers. Some were pinching the cheeks of the apples to make them red, and others were reeling silk for the corn-tassels. Then Frey looked down upon the earth, where men were scurrying around like little ants, improving the blessings which his servants were sending, and often stopping their work to give thanks to their beloved Frey. And this made his kind heart glad.

Next he turned his gaze down into the depths of the blue ocean which flowed about Midgard like a great river. And down in the sea-caves he saw the mermaids playing, Queen Ran and her daughters the white-capped Waves, with their nets ready to catch the sailors who might be drowned at sea. And he saw King Œgir, among the whales and dolphins, with all the myriad wondrous creatures who lived in his watery empire. But Frey's father, old Niörd, lord of the ocean wind, would have been more interested than he in such a sight.

Last of all Frey bent his eyes upon the far, cold land of Jotunheim, beyond the ocean, where the giants lived; and as he did so, a beam of brightness dazzled him. He rubbed his eyes and looked again; and lo! the flash was from the bright arms of a beautiful maiden, who was passing from her father's hall to her own little bower. When she raised her arms to open the door, the air and water reflected their brightness so that the whole world was flooded with light, and one shaft shot straight into the heart of Frey,

making him love her and long for her more than for anything he had ever seen. But because he knew that she
must be a giant's daughter, how could he win her for his
bride? Frey descended from Odin's throne very sadly,
very hopelessly, and went home with a heavy heart which
would let him neither eat nor sleep. This was the penalty
which came for his disobedience in presuming to sit upon
Odin's sacred throne.

For hours no one dared speak to Frey, he looked so
gloomy and forbidding, quite unlike his own gay self.
Niörd his father was greatly worried, and knew not what
to do; at last he sent for Skirnir, who was Frey's favorite
servant, and bade him find out what was the matter.
Skirnir therefore went to his master, whom he found sitting all alone in his great hall, looking as if there were no
more joy for him.

"What ails you, master?" asked Skirnir. "From the beginning of time when we were very young we two have lived
together, and I have served you with loving care. You
ought, then, to have confidence in me and tell me all your
troubles."

"Ah, Skirnir, my faithful friend," sighed Frey, "how shall
I tell you my sorrow? The sun shines every day, but no
longer brings light to my sad heart. And all because I saw
more than was good for me!"

So then he told Skirnir all the matter: how he had stolen
into Odin's seat, and what he had seen from there; how he
loved a giant's daughter whose arms were more bright
than silver moonbeams.

"Oh, Skirnir, I love her very dearly," he cried; "but
because our races are enemies she would never marry
me, I know, even if her father would allow it. Therefore is
it that I am so sad."

But Skirnir did not seem to think the case so hopeless.
"Give me but your swift horse," he said, "which can bear
me even through flames of fire and thick smoke; give me
also your magic wand and your sword, which, if he be

brave who carries it, will smite by itself any giant who comes in its way,—and I will see what I can do for you."

Then Skirnir rode forth upon his dangerous errand; for a visit to Giant Land was ever a perilous undertaking, as you may well imagine. As Skirnir rode, he patted his good horse's neck and said to him, "Dark it is, friend, and we have to go over frosty mountains and among frosty people this night. Bear me well, good horse; for if you fail me the giants will catch us both, and neither of us will return to bring the news to our master Frey."

After a long night of hard riding over mountain and desolate snowfield, Skirnir came to that part of Jotunheim where the giant Gymir dwelt. This was the father of Gerd, the maiden whom Frey had seen and loved. But first he had to ride through a hedge of flame, which the horse passed bravely. Now when he came to the house of Gymir, he found a pack of fierce dogs chained about the door to keep strangers away.

"H'm!" thought Skirnir, "I like this little indeed. I must find out whether there be not some other entrance." So he looked around, and soon he saw a herdsman sitting on a little hill, tending his cattle. Skirnir rode up to him.

"Ho, friend," he cried. "Tell me, how am I to pass these growling curs so that I may speak with the young maiden who dwells in this house?"

"Are you mad, or are you a spirit who is not afraid of death!" exclaimed the herdsman. "Know you not that you can never enter there? That is Gymir's dwelling, and he lets no one speak with his fair and good daughter."

"If I choose to die, you need not weep for me," quoth Skirnir boldly. "But I do not think that I am yet to die. The Norn-maidens spun my fate centuries ago, and they only can tell what is to be." Now Skirnir's voice was loud and the hoof-beats of his horse were mighty. For this was one of the magic steeds of Asgard, used to bearing Frey himself on his broad back. And not without much noise had all these things been said and done. From her room in

Gymir's mansion Gerd heard the stranger's voice, and to her waiting-maid she said, "What are these sounds that I hear? The earth is trembling and all the house shakes."

Then the servant ran to look out of the window, and in a minute she popped in her head, crying, "Here is a mighty stranger who has dismounted from his horse and leads him by the bridle to crop the grass."

Gerd was curious to see who this stranger might be; for her father kept her close and she saw few visitors.

"Bid him enter our hall," she said, "and give him a horn of bright mead to drink. I will see him, though I fear it is the slayer of my brother." For Gerd was the sister of Thiasse whom Thor slew.

So Skirnir came into the hall, and Gerd received him coldly. "Who are you?" she asked. "Which of the wise Æsir are you? For I know that only one of the mighty ones from Asgard would have the courage and the power to pass through the raging flames that surround my father's land."

"I come from Frey, O maiden," said Skirnir, "from Frey, whom all folk love. I come to beg that you also will love him and consent to be his wife. For Frey has seen your beauty, and you are very dear to him."

Gerd laughed carelessly. "I have heard of your fair Frey," she said, "and how he is more dear to all than sunshine and the sweet smell of flowers. But he is not dear to me. I do not wish the love of Frey, nor any of that race of giant-killers. Tell him that I will not be his bride."

"Stay, be not so hasty," urged Skirnir. "We have more words to exchange before I start for home. Look, I will give you eleven golden apples from Asgard's magic tree if you will go with me to Frey's dwelling."

Gerd would hear nothing of the golden apples. Then Skirnir promised her the golden ring, Draupnir, which the dwarfs had made for Odin, out of which every ninth night dropped eight other rings as large and bright. But neither would Gerd listen to word of this generous gift. "I have gold enough in my father's house," she said disdainfully.

"With such trifles you cannot tempt me to marry your Frey."

Then Skirnir was very angry, and he began to storm and threaten. "I will strike you with the bright sword which I hold in my hand!" he cried. "It is Frey's magic sword, under which even that stout old giant your father must sink if he comes within its reach." But again Gerd laughed, though with less mirth in her laughter. "I will tame you with Frey's magic wand!" he threatened, "the wand with which he rules the Light-Elves, and changes folk into strange shapes. You shall vanish from the sight of men, and pass your life on the eagle's mount far above the sky, where you shall sit all day, too sad to eat. And when you come thence, after countless ages, you will be a hideous monster at which all creatures will stare in mockery and scorn."

These were dreadful words, and Gerd no longer laughed when she heard them. But she was obstinate. "I do not love Frey," she said, "and I will not be his bride."

Then Skirnir was angry indeed, and his fury blazed out in threats most horrible. "If you will not marry my dear master," he cried, "you shall be the most unhappy girl that ever lived. You shall cry all day long and never see joy again. You shall marry a hideous old three-headed giant, and from day to day you shall ever be in terror of some still more dreadful fate to come!"

Now Gerd began to tremble, for she saw that Frey's servant meant every word that he spoke. But she was not ready to yield. "Go back to the land of Elves," she taunted; "I will not be their Queen at any cost."

Now Skirnir grasped the magic wand, and waving it over her, spoke his last words of threat and anger. "The gods are angry with you, evil maiden!" he cried, "Odin sees your obstinacy from his throne, and will punish you for your cruelty to kind Frey. Frey himself, instead of loving, will shun you when the gods arm themselves to destroy you and all your race. Listen, Giants, Dwarfs, Light-Elves, Men, and all friends of the Æsir! I forbid any one to have aught to do with this wicked girl,—only the old giant who shall carry her to his gloomy castle, barred and bolted and grated across. Misery, pain, and madness—this, Gerd, is the fate which I wave over you with my wand, unless speedily you repent and do my will."

Poor Gerd gasped and trembled under this dreadful doom. Her willfulness was quite broken, and now she sought only to make Skirnir unsay the words of horror. "Hold!" she cried; "be welcome, youth, in the name of your powerful master, Frey. I cannot afford to be enemy of such as he. Drink this icy cup of welcome filled with the giant's mead, and take with it my consent to be the bride of Frey. But alas! I never thought to be a friend to one of Asgard's race."

"You shall never repent, fair Gerd," said Skirnir gently. For now that he had won his will, he was all smiles and friendliness. "And when you see my dear master, you will be glad indeed that you did not insist upon wedding the old three-headed giant. For Frey is fair,—ay, as fair as are you yourself. And that is saying much, sweet lady."

So Gerd promised that in nine days she would come to be the bride of Frey. And the more she thought it over, the less unpleasant seemed the idea. So that before the time was passed, she was almost as eager as Frey for their happy meeting; not quite so eager, for you must remember that she had not yet seen him and knew not all his glory, while he knew what it was to long and long for what he had once seen.

Indeed, when Skirnir galloped back to Frey as fast as the good horse could take him, still Frey chided him for being slow. And when the faithful fellow told the good news of the bride who was to be his master's in nine short days, still Frey frowned and grumbled impatiently.

"How can I wait to see her?" he cried. "One day is long; two days are a century; nine days seem forever. Oh, Skirnir, could you not have done better than that for your dear master?"

But Skirnir forgave Frey for his impatience, for he knew

that thenceforward his master would love all the better him who had done so nobly to win the beloved bride.

When Gerd married Frey and went with him to live in Elf Land, where he and she were king and queen, they were the happiest folk that the world ever saw. And Gerd was as grateful to Skirnir as Frey himself. For she could not help thinking of that dreadful old three-headed giant whom but for him she might have married, instead of her beautiful, kind Frey.

So you see that sometimes one is happier in the end if she is not allowed to have her own way.

Thor's Visit to the Giants

Nowadays, since their journey to get the stolen hammer, Thor and Loki were good friends, for Loki seemed to have turned over a new leaf and to be a very decent sort of fellow; but really he was the same sly rascal at heart, only biding his time for mischief. However, in this tale he behaves well enough.

It was a long time since Thor had slain any giants, and he was growing restless for an adventure. "Come, Loki," he said one day, "let us fare forth to Giant Land and see what news there is among the Big Folk."

Loki laughed, saying, "Let us go, Thor. I know I am safe with you"; which was a piece of flattery that happened to be true.

So they mounted the goat chariot as they had done so many times before and rumbled away out of Asgard. All day they rode; and when evening came they stopped at a little house on the edge of a forest, where lived a poor peasant with his wife, his son, and daughter.

"May we rest here for the night, friend?" asked Thor; and noting their poverty, he added, "We bring our own supper, and ask but a bed to sleep in." So the peasant was glad to have them stay. Then Thor, who knew what he was about, killed and cooked his two goats, and invited the family of peasants to sup with him and Loki; but when the meal was ended, he bade them carefully save all the bones and throw them into the goatskins which he had laid beside the hearth. Then Thor and Loki lay down to sleep.

In the morning, very early, before the rest were awake, Thor rose, and taking his hammer, Miölnir, went into the kitchen, where were the remains of his faithful goats. Now the magic hammer was skillful, not only to slay, but to restore, when Thor's hand wielded it. He touched with it the two heaps of skin and bones, and lo! up sprang the goats, alive and well, and as good as new. No, not quite as good as new. What was this? Thor roared with anger, for one of the goats was lame in one of his legs, and limped sorely. "Some one has meddled with the bones!" he cried. "Who has touched the bones that I bade be kept so carefully?"

Thialfi, the peasant's son, had broken one of the thighbones in order to get at the sweet marrow, and this Thor soon discovered by the lad's guilty face; then Thor was angry indeed. His knuckles grew white as he clenched the handle of Miölnir, ready to hurl it and destroy the whole unlucky house and family; but the peasant and the other three fell upon their knees, trembling with fear, and begged him to spare them. They offered him all that they owned,—they offered even to become his slaves,—if he would but spare their wretched lives.

They looked so miserable that Thor was sorry for them, and resolved at last to punish them only by taking away Thialfi, the son, and Röskva, the daughter, thenceforth to be his servants. And this was not so bad a bargain for Thor, for Thialfi was the swiftest of foot of any man in the whole world.

So he left the goats behind, and fared forth with his three attendants straight towards the east and Jotunheim. Thialfi carried Thor's wallet with their scanty store of food. They crossed the sea and came at last to a great forest, through which they tramped all day, until once more it was night; and now they must find a place in which all could sleep safely until morning. They wandered about here and there, looking for some sign of a dwelling, and at last they came to a big, queer-shaped house. Very queer indeed it was; for the door at one end was as broad as the house itself! They entered, and lay down to sleep; but at midnight Thor was wakened by a terrible noise. The ground shook under them like an earthquake, and the house trembled as if it would fall to pieces. Thor arose and called to his companions that there was danger about, and that they must be on guard. Groping in the dark, they found a long, narrow chamber on the right, where Loki and the two peasants hid trembling, while Thor guarded the doorway, hammer in hand. All night long the terrible noises continued, and Thor's attendants were frightened almost to death; but early in the morning Thor stole forth to find out what it all meant. And lo! close at hand in the forest lay an enormous giant, sound asleep and snoring loudly. Then Thor understood whence all their night's terror had proceeded, for the giant was so huge that his snoring shook even the trees of the forest, and made the mountains tremble. So much the better! Here at last was a giant for Thor to tackle. He buckled his belt of power more tightly to increase his strength, and laid hold of Miölnir to hurl it at the giant's forehead; but just at that moment the giant waked, rose slowly to his feet, and stood staring mildly at Thor. He did not seem a fierce giant, so Thor did not kill him at once. "Who are you?" asked Thor sturdily.

"I am the giant Skrymir, little fellow," answered the stranger, "and well I know who you are, Thor of Asgard. But what have you been doing with my glove?"

Then the giant stooped and picked up—what do you think?—the queer house in which Thor and his three companions had spent the night! Loki and the two others had run out of their chamber in affright when they felt it lifted; and their chamber was the thumb of the giant's glove. That was a giant indeed, and Thor felt sure that they must be well upon their way to Giant Land.

When Skrymir learned where they were going, he asked

if he might not wend with them, and Thor said that he was willing. Now Skrymir untied his wallet and sat down under a tree to eat his breakfast, while Thor and his party chose another place, not far away, for their picnic. When all had finished, the giant said, "Let us put our provisions together in one bag, my friends, and I will carry it for you." This seemed fair enough, for Thor had so little food left that he was not afraid to risk losing it; so he agreed, and Skrymir tied all the provisions in his bag and strode on before them with enormous strides, so fast that even Thialfi could scarcely keep up with him.

The day passed, and late in the evening Skrymir halted under a great oak-tree, saying, "Let us rest here. I must have a nap, and you must have your dinner. Here is the wallet,—open it and help yourselves." Then he lay down on the moss, and was soon snoring lustily.

Thor tried to open the wallet, in vain; he could not loosen a single knot of the huge thongs that fastened it. He strained and tugged, growing angrier and redder after every useless attempt. This was too much; the giant was making him appear absurd before his servants. He seized his hammer, and bracing his feet with all his might, struck Skrymir a blow on his head. Skrymir stirred lazily, yawned, opened one eye, and asked whether a leaf had fallen on his forehead, and whether his companions had dined yet. Thor bit his lip with vexation, but he answered that they were ready for bed; so he and his three followers retired to rest under another oak.

But Thor did not sleep that night. He lay thinking how he had been put to shame, and how Loki had snickered at the sight of Thor's vain struggles with the giant's wallet, and he resolved that it should not happen again. At about midnight, once more he heard the giant's snore resounding like thunder through the forest. Thor arose, clenching Miölnir tight, and stole over to the tree where Skrymir slept; then with all his might he hurled the hammer and struck the giant on the crown of his head, so hard that the hammer sank deep into his skull. At this the giant awoke with a start, exclaiming, "What is that? Did an acorn fall on my head? What are you doing there, Thor?"

Thor stepped back quickly, answering that he had waked up, but that it was only midnight, so they might all sleep some hours longer. "If I can only give him one more blow before morning," he thought, "he will never see daylight again." So he lay watching until Skrymir had fallen asleep once more, which was near daybreak; then Thor arose as before, and going very softly to the giant's side, smote him on the temple so sore that the hammer sank into his skull up to the very handle. "Surely, he is killed now," thought Thor.

But Skrymir only raised himself on his elbow, stroked his chin, and said, "There are birds above me in the tree. Methinks that just now a feather fell upon my head. What, Thor! are you awake? I am afraid you slept but poorly this night. Come, now, it is high time to rise and make ready for the day. You are not far from our giant city,—Utgard we call it. Aha! I have heard you whispering together. You think that I am big; but you will see fellows taller still when you come to Utgard. And now I have a piece of advice to give you. Do not pride yourselves overmuch upon your importance. The followers of Utgard's king think little of such manikins as you, and will not bear any nonsense, I assure you. Be advised; return homeward before it is too late. If you will go on, however, your way lies there to the eastward. Yonder is my path, over the mountains to the north."

So saying, Skrymir hoisted his wallet upon his shoulders, and turning back upon the path that led into the forest, left them staring after him and hoping that they might never see his big bulk again.

Thor and his companions journeyed on until noon, when they saw in the distance a great city, on a lofty plain. As they came nearer, they found the buildings so high that the travelers had to bend back their necks in order to see the tops. "This must be Utgard, the giant city," said Thor.

And Utgard indeed it was. At the entrance was a great barred gate, locked so that no one might enter. It was useless to try to force a passage in; even Thor's great strength could not move it on its hinges. But it was a giant gate, and the bars were made to keep out other giants, with no thought of folk so small as these who now were bent upon finding entrance by one way or another. It was not dignified, and noble Thor disliked the idea. Yet it was their only way; so one by one they squeezed and wriggled between the bars, until they stood in a row inside. In front of them was a wonderful great hall with the door wide open. Thor and the three entered, and found themselves in the midst of a company of giants, the very hugest of their kind. At the end of the hall sat the king upon an enormous throne. Thor, who had been in giant companies ere now, went straight up to the throne and greeted the king with civil words. But the giant merely glanced at him with a disagreeable smile, and said,—

"It is wearying to ask travelers about their journey. Such little fellows as you four can scarcely have had any adventures worth mentioning. Stay, now! Do I guess aright? Is this manikin Thor of Asgard, or no? Ah, no! I have heard of Thor's might. You cannot really be he, unless you are taller than you seem, and stronger too. Let us see what feats you and your companions can perform to amuse us. No one is allowed here who cannot excel others in some way or another. What can you do best?"

At this word, Loki, who had entered last, spoke up readily: "There is one thing that I can do,—I can eat faster than any man." For Loki was famished with hunger, and thought he saw a way to win a good meal.

Then the king answered, "Truly, that is a noble accomplishment of yours, if you can prove your words true. Let us make the test." So he called forth from among his men Logi,—whose name means "fire,"—and bade him match his powers with the stranger.

Now a trough full of meat was set upon the floor, with Loki at one end of it and the giant Logi at the other. Each began to gobble the meat as fast as he could, and it was not a pretty sight to see them. Midway in the trough they met, and at first it would seem as if neither had beaten the other. Loki had indeed done wondrous well in eating the meat from the bones so fast; but Logi, the giant, had in the same time eaten not only meat but bones also, and had swallowed his half of the trough into the bargain. Loki was vanquished at his own game, and retired looking much ashamed and disgusted.

The king then pointed at Thialfi, and asked what that young man could best do. Thialfi answered that of all men he was the swiftest runner, and that he was not afraid to race with any one whom the king might select.

"That is a goodly craft," said the king, smiling; "but you must be a swift runner indeed if you can win a race from my Hugi. Let us go to the racing-ground."

They followed him out to the plain where Hugi, whose name means "thought," was ready to race with young Thialfi. In the first run Hugi came in so far ahead that when he reached the goal he turned about and went back to meet Thialfi. "You must do better than that, Thialfi, if you hope to win," said the king, laughing, "though I must allow that no one ever before came here who could run so fast as you."

They ran a second race; and this time when Hugi reached the goal there was a long bow-shot between him and Thialfi.

"You are truly a good runner," exclaimed the king. "I doubt not that no man can race like you; but you cannot win from my giant lad, I think. The last time shall show." Then they ran for the third time, and Thialfi put forth all his strength, speeding like the wind; but all his skill was in vain. Hardly had he reached the middle of the course when he heard the shouts of the giants announcing that Hugi had won the goal. Thialfi, too, was beaten at his own game, and he withdrew, as Loki had done, shamefaced and sulky.

There remained now only Thor to redeem the honor of

his party, for Röskva the maiden was useless here. Thor had watched the result of these trials with surprise and anger, though he knew it was no fault of Loki or of Thialfi that they had been worsted by the giants. And Thor was resolved to better even his own former great deeds. The king called to Thor, and asked him what he thought he could best do to prove himself as mighty as the stories told of him. Thor answered that he would undertake to drink more mead than any one of the king's men. At this proposal the king laughed aloud, as if it were a giant joke. He summoned his cup-bearer to fetch his horn of punishment, out of which the giants were wont to drink in turn. And when they returned to the hall, the great vessel was brought to the king.

"When any one empties this horn at one draught, we call him a famous drinker," said the king. "Some of my men empty it in two trials; but no one is so poor a manikin that he cannot empty it in three. Take the horn, Thor, and see what you can do with it."

Now Thor was very thirsty, so he seized the horn eagerly. It did not seem to him so very large, for he had drunk from other mighty vessels ere now. But indeed, it was deep. He raised it to his lips and took a long pull, saying to himself, "There! I have emptied it already, I know." Yet when he set the horn down to see how well he had done, he found that he seemed scarcely to have drained a drop; the horn was brimming as before. The king chuckled.

"Well, you have drunk but little," he said. "I would never have believed that famous Thor would lower the horn so soon. But doubtless you will finish all at a second draught."

Instead of answering, Thor raised the horn once more to his lips, resolved to do better than before. But for some reason the tip of the horn seemed hard to raise, and when he set the vessel down again his heart sank, for he feared that he had drunk even less than at his first trial. Yet he had really done better, for now it was easy to carry the horn without spilling. The king smiled grimly. "How now,

Thor!" he cried. "You have left too much for your third
trial. I fear you will never be able to empty the little horn
in three draughts, as the least of my men can do. Ho, ho!
You will not be thought so great a hero here as the folk
deem you in Asgard, if you cannot play some other game
more skillfully than you do this one."

At this speech Thor grew very angry. He raised the horn
to his mouth and drank lustily, as long as he was able. But
when he looked into the horn, he found that some drops
still remained. He had not been able to empty it in three
draughts. Angrily he flung down the horn, and said that he
would have no more of it.

"Ah, Master Thor," taunted the king, "it is now plain that
you are not so mighty as we thought you. Are you inclined
to try some other feats? For indeed, you are easily beaten
at this one."

"I will try whatever you like," said Thor; "but your horn
is a wondrous one, and among the Æsir such a draught as
mine would be called far from little. Come, now,—what
game do you next propose, O King?"

The king thought a moment, then answered carelessly,
"There is a little game with which my youngsters amuse
themselves, though it is so simple as to be almost child-
ish. It is merely the exercise of lifting my cat from the
ground. I should never have dared suggest such a feat as
this to you, Thor of Asgard, had I not seen that great tasks
are beyond your skill. It may be that you will find this hard
enough." So he spoke, smiling slyly, and at that moment
there came stalking into the hall a monstrous gray cat,
with eyes of yellow fire.

"Ho! Is this the creature I am to lift?" queried Thor. And
when they said that it was, he seized the cat around its
gray, huge body and tugged with all his might to lift it from
the floor. Then the wretched cat, lengthening and lengthening, arched its back like the span of a bridge; and
though Thor tugged and heaved his best, he could manage to lift but one of its huge feet off the floor. The other
three remained as firmly planted as iron pillars.

"Oho, oho!" laughed the king, delighted at this sight. "It is just as I thought it would be. Poor little Thor! My cat is too big for him."

"Little I may seem in this land of monsters," cried Thor wrathfully, "but now let him who dares come hither and try a hug with me."

"Nay, little Thor," said the king, seeking to make him yet more angry, "there is not one of my men who would wrestle with you. Why, they would call it child's play, my little fellow. But, for the joke of it, call in my old foster-mother, Elli. She has wrestled with and worsted many a man who seemed no weaker than you, O Thor. She shall try a fall with you."

Now in came the old crone, Elli, whose very name meant "age." She was wrinkled and gray, and her back was bent nearly double with the weight of the years which she carried, but she chuckled when she saw Thor standing with bared arm in the middle of the floor. "Come and be thrown, dearie," she cried in her cracked voice, grinning horribly.

"I will not wrestle with a woman!" exclaimed Thor, eyeing her with pity and disgust, for she was an ugly creature to behold. But the old woman taunted him to his face and the giants clapped their hands, howling that he was "afraid." So there was no way but that Thor must grapple with the hag.

The game began. Thor rushed at the old woman and gripped her tightly in his iron arms, thinking that as soon as she screamed with the pain of his mighty hug, he would give over. But the crone seemed not to mind it at all. Indeed, the more he crushed her old ribs together the firmer and stronger she stood. Now in her turn the witch attempted to trip up Thor's heels, and it was wonderful to see her power and agility. Thor soon began to totter, great Thor, in the hands of a poor old woman! He struggled hard, he braced himself, he turned and twisted. It was no use; the old woman's arms were as strong as knotted oak. In a few moments Thor sank upon one knee, and that was a sign that he was beaten. The king signaled for them to stop. "You need wrestle no more, Thor," he said, with a curl to his lip, "we see what sort of fellow you are. I thought that old Elli would have no difficulty in bringing to his knees him who could not lift my cat. But come, now, night is almost here. We will think no more of contests. You and your companions shall sup with us as welcome guests and bide here till the morrow."

Now as soon as the king had pleased himself in proving how small and weak were these strangers who had come to the giant city, he became very gracious and kind. But you can fancy whether or no Thor and the others had a good appetite for the banquet where all the giants ate so merrily. You can fancy whether or no they were happy when they went to bed after the day of defeats, and you can guess what sweet dreams they had.

The next morning at daybreak the four guests arose and made ready to steal back to Asgard without attracting any more attention. For this adventure alone of all those in which Thor had taken part had been a disgraceful failure. Silently and with bowed heads they were slipping away from the hall when the king himself came to them and begged them to stay.

"You shall not leave Utgard without breakfast," he said kindly, "nor would I have you depart feeling unfriendly to me."

Then he ordered a goodly breakfast for the travelers, with store of choicest dainties for them to eat and drink. When the four had broken fast, he escorted them to the city gate where they were to say farewell. But at the last moment he turned to Thor with a sly, strange smile and asked,—

"Tell me now truly, brother Thor; what think you of your visit to the giant city? Do you feel as mighty a fellow as you did before you entered our gates, or are you satisfied that there are folk even sturdier than yourself?"

At this question Thor flushed scarlet, and the lightning

flashed angrily in his eye. Briefly enough he answered that he must confess to small pride in his last adventure, for that his visit to the king had been full of shame to the hero of Asgard. "My name will become a joke among your people," quoth he. "You will call me Thor the puny little fellow, which vexes me more than anything; for I have not been wont to blush at my name."

Then the king looked at him frankly, pleased with the humble manner of Thor's speech. "Nay," he said slowly, "hang not your head so shamedly, brave Thor. You have not done so ill as you think. Listen, I have somewhat to tell you, now that you are outside Utgard,—which, if I live, you shall never enter again. Indeed, you should not have entered at all had I guessed what noble strength was really yours,— strength which very nearly brought me and my whole city to destruction."

To these words Thor and his companions listened with open-mouthed astonishment. What could the king mean, they wondered? The giant continued:—

"By magic alone were you beaten, Thor. Of magic alone were my triumphs,—not real, but seeming to be so. Do you remember the giant Skrymir whom you found sleeping and snoring in the forest? That was I. I learned your errand and resolved to lower your pride. When you vainly strove to untie my wallet, you did not know that I had fastened it with invisible iron wire, in order that you might be baffled by the knots. Thrice you struck me with your hammer,—ah! what mighty blows were those! The least one would have killed me, had it fallen on my head as you deemed it did. In my hall is a rock with three square hollows in it, one of them deeper than the others. These are the dents of your wondrous hammer, my Thor. For, while you thought I slept, I slipped the rock under the hammer-strokes, and into this hard crust Miölnir bit. Ha, ha! It was a pretty jest."

Now Thor's brow was growing black at this tale of the giant's trickery, but at the same time he held up his head and seemed less ashamed of his weakness, knowing now that it had been no weakness, but lack of guile. He listened frowningly for the rest of the tale. The king went on:—

"When you came to my city, still it was magic that worsted your party at every turn. Loki was certainly the hungriest fellow I ever saw, and his deeds at the trencher were marvelous to behold. But the Logi who ate with him was Fire, and easily enough fire can consume your meat, bones, and wood itself. Thialfi, my boy, you are a runner swift as the wind. Never before saw I such a race as yours. But the Hugi who ran with you was Thought, my thought. And who can keep pace with the speed of winged thought? Next, Thor, it was your turn to show your might. Bravely indeed you strove. My heart is sick with envy of your strength and skill. But they availed you naught against my magic. When you drank from the long horn, thinking you had done so ill, in truth you had performed a miracle,—never thought I to behold the like. You guessed not that the end of the horn was out in the ocean, which no one might drain dry. Yet, mighty one, the draughts you swallowed have lowered the tide upon the shore. Henceforth at certain times the sea will ebb; and this is by great Thor's drinking. The cat also which you almost lifted,—it was no cat, but the great Midgard serpent himself who encircles the whole world. He had barely length enough for his head and tail to touch in a circle about the sea. But you raised him so high that he almost touched heaven. How terrified we were when we saw you heave one of his mighty feet from the ground! For who could tell what horror might happen had you raised him bodily. Ah, and your wrestling with old Elli! That was the most marvelous act of all. You had nearly overthrown Age itself; yet there has never lived one, nor will such ever be found, whom Elli, old age, will not cast to earth at last. So you were beaten, Thor, but by a mere trick. Ha, ha! How angry you looked,—I shall never forget! But now we must part, and I think you see that it will be best for both of us that we should not meet again. As I have done once, so can I always protect my city by magic spells. Yes, should you come again to visit us, even better prepared than now, yet you could never do us serious harm. Yet the wear and tear upon the nerves of both of us is something not lightly forgotten."

He ceased, smiling pleasantly, but with a threatening look in his eye. Thor's wrath had been slowly rising during this tedious, grim speech, and he could control it no longer.

"Cheat and trickster!" he cried, "your wiles shall avail you nothing now that I know your true self. You have put me to shame, now my hammer shall shame you beyond all reckoning!" and he raised Miölnir to smite the giant deathfully. But at that moment the king faded before his very eyes. And when he turned to look for the giant city that he might destroy it,—as he had so many giant dwellings,—there was in the place where it had been but a broad, fair plain, with no sign of any palace, wall, or gate. Utgard had vanished. The king had kept one trick of magic for the last.

Then Thor and his three companions wended their way back to Asgard. But they were slower than usual about answering questions concerning their last adventure, their wondrous visit to the giant city. Truth to tell, magic or no magic, Thor and Loki had showed but a poor figure that day. For the first time in all their meeting with Thor the giants had not come off any the worse for the encounter. Perhaps it was a lesson that he sorely needed. I am afraid that he was rather inclined to think well of himself. But then, he had reason, had he not?

Thor's Fishing

Once upon a time the Æsir went to take dinner with old Œgir, the king of the ocean. Down under the green waves they went to the coral palace where Œgir lived with his wife, Queen Ran, and his daughters, the Waves. But Œgir was not expecting so large a party to dinner, and he had not mead enough for them all to drink. "I must brew some more mead," he said to himself. But when he came to look for a kettle in which to make the brew, there was none in all the sea large enough for the purpose. At first Œgir did not know what to do; but at last he decided to consult the gods themselves, for he knew how wise and powerful his guests were, and he hoped that they might help him to a kettle.

Now when he told the Æsir his trouble they were much interested, for they were hungry and thirsty, and longed for some of Œgir's good mead. "Where can we find a kettle?" they said to one another. "Who has a kettle huge enough to hold mead for all the Æsir?"

Then Týr the brave turned to Thor with a grand idea. "My father, the giant Hymir, has such a kettle," he said. "I have seen it often in his great palace near Elivâgar, the river of ice. This famous kettle is a mile deep, and surely that is large enough to brew all the mead we may need."

"Surely, surely it is large enough," laughed Œgir. "But how are we to get the kettle, my distinguished guests? Who will go to Giant Land to fetch the kettle a mile deep?"

"That will I," said brave Thor. "I will go to Hymir's

dwelling and bring thence the little kettle, if Týr will go
with me to show me the way." So Thor and Týr set out
together for the land of snow and ice, where the giant
Hymir lived. They traveled long and they traveled fast,
and finally they came to the huge house which had once
been Týr 's home, before he went to live with the good
folk in Asgard.

Well Týr knew the way to enter, and it was not long
before they found themselves in the hall of Hymir's
dwelling, peering about for some sign of the kettle which
they had come so far to seek; and sure enough, presently
they discovered eight huge kettles hanging in a row from
one of the beams in the ceiling. While the two were wondering which kettle might be the one they sought, there
came in Týr 's grandmother,—and a terrible grandmother
she was. No wonder that Týr had run away from home
when he was very little; for this dreadful creature was a
giantess with nine hundred heads, each more ugly than the
others, and her temper was as bad as were her looks. She
began to roar and bellow; and no one knows what this evil
old person would have done to her grandson and his friend
had not there come into the hall at this moment another
woman, fair and sweet, and glittering with golden orna-
ments. This was Týr's good mother, who loved him dearly,
and who had mourned his absence during long years.

With a cry of joy she threw herself upon her son's neck,
bidding him welcome forty times over. She welcomed
Thor also when she found out who he was; but she sent
away the wicked old grandmother, that she might not
hear, for Thor's name was not dear to the race of giants,
to so many of whom he had brought dole and death.

"Why have you come, dear son, after so many years?"
she cried. "I know that some great undertaking calls you
and this noble fellow to your father's hall. Danger and
death wait here for such as you and he; and only some
quest with glory for its reward could have brought you

to such risks. Tell me your secret, Tŷr, and I will not betray it."

Then they told her how that they had come to carry away the giant kettle; and Tŷr's mother promised that she would help them all she could. But she warned them that it would be dangerous indeed, for that Hymir had been in a terrible temper for many days, and that the very sight of a stranger made him wild with rage. Hastily she gave them meat and drink, for they were nearly famished after their long journey; and then she looked around to see where she should hide them against Hymir's return, who was now away at the hunt.

"Aha!" she cried. "The very thing! You shall bide in the great kettle itself; and if you escape Hymir's terrible eye, it may hap that you will find a way to make off with your hiding-place, which is what you want." So the kind creature helped them to climb into the great kettle where it hung from one of the rafters in a row with seven others; but this one was the biggest and the strongest of them all.

Hardly had they snuggled down out of sight when Tŷr's mother began to tremble. "Hist!" she cried. "I hear him coming. Keep as still as ever you can, O Tŷr and Thor!" The floor also began to tremble, and the eight kettles to clatter against one another, as Hymir's giant footsteps approached the house. Outside they could hear the icebergs shaking with a sound like thunder; indeed, the whole earth quivered as if with fear when the terrible giant Hymir strode home from the hunt. He came into the hall puffing and blowing, and immediately the air of the room grew chilly; for his beard was hung with icicles and his face was frosted hard, while his breath was a winter wind,—a freezing blast.

"Ho! wife," he growled, "what news, what news? For I see by the footprints in the snow outside that you have had visitors to-day."

Then indeed the poor woman trembled; but she tried not to look frightened as she answered, "Yes, you have a guest, O Hymir!—a guest whom you have long wished to see. Your son Tŷr has returned to visit his father's hall."

"Humph!" growled Hymir, with a terrible frown. "Whom has he brought here with him, the rascal? There are prints of two persons' feet in the snow. Come, wife, tell me all; for I shall soon find out the truth, whether or no."

"He has brought a friend of his,—a dear friend, O Hymir!" faltered the mother. "Surely, our son's friends are welcome when he brings them to this our home, after so long an absence."

But Hymir howled with rage at the word "friend." "Where are they hidden?" he cried. "Friend, indeed! It is one of those bloody fellows from Asgard, I know,—one of those giant-killers whom my good mother taught me to hate with all my might. Let me get at him! Tell me instantly where he is hidden, or I will pull down the hall about your ears!"

Now when the wicked old giant spoke like this, his wife knew that he must be obeyed. Still she tried to put off the fateful moment of the discovery. "They are standing over there behind that pillar," she said. Instantly Hymir glared at the pillar towards which she pointed, and at his frosty glance—snick-snack!—the marble pillar cracked in two, and down crashed the great roof-beam which held the eight kettles. Smash! went the kettles; and there they lay shivered into little pieces at Hymir's feet,—all except one, the largest of them all, and that was the kettle in which Thor and Tŷr lay hidden, scarcely daring to breathe lest the giant should guess where they were. Tŷr's mother screamed when she saw the big kettle fall with the others: but when she found that this one, alone of them all, lay on its side unbroken, because it was so tough and strong, she held her breath to see what would happen next.

And what happened was this: out stepped Thor and Tŷr, and making low bows to Hymir, they stood side by side, smiling and looking as unconcerned as if they really enjoyed all this hubbub; and I dare say that they did indeed, being Týr the bold and Thor the thunderer, who had been in Giant Land many times ere this.

Hymir gave scarcely a glance at his son, but he eyed Thor with a frown of hatred and suspicion, for he knew that this was one of Father Odin's brave family, though he could not tell which one. However, he thought best to be civil, now that Thor was actually before him. So with gruff politeness he invited the two guests to supper.

Now Thor was a valiant fellow at the table as well as in war, as you remember; and at sight of the good things on the board his eyes sparkled. Three roast oxen there were upon the giant's table, and Thor fell to with a will and finished two of them himself! You should have seen the giant stare.

"Truly, friend, you have a goodly appetite," he said. "You have eaten all the meat that I have in my larder; and if you dine with us to-morrow, I must insist that you catch your own dinner of fish. I cannot undertake to provide food for such an appetite!"

Now this was not hospitable of Hymir, but Thor did not mind. "I like well to fish, good Hymir," he laughed; "and when you fare forth with your boat in the morning, I will go with you and see what I can find for my dinner at the bottom of the sea."

When the morning came, the giant made ready for the fishing, and Thor rose early to go with him.

"Ho, Hymir," exclaimed Thor, "have you bait enough for us both?"

Hymir answered gruffly, "You must dig your own bait when you go fishing with me. I have no time to waste on you, sirrah."

Then Thor looked about to see what he could use for bait; and presently he spied a herd of Hymir's oxen feeding in the meadow. "Aha! just the thing!" he cried; and seizing the hugest ox of all, he trotted down to the shore with it under his arm, as easily as you would carry a handful of clams for bait. When Hymir saw this, he was very angry. He pushed the boat off from shore and began to row away as fast as he could, so that Thor might not have a chance to come aboard. But Thor made one long step and planted himself snugly in the stern of the boat.

"No, no, brother Hymir," he said, laughing. "You invited me to go fishing, and a-fishing I will go; for I have my bait, and my hope is high that great luck I shall see this day." So he took an oar and rowed mightily in the stern, while Hymir the giant rowed mightily at the prow; and no one ever saw boat skip over the water so fast as this one did on the day when these two big fellows went fishing together.

Far and fast they rowed, until they came to a spot where Hymir cried, "Hold! Let us anchor here and fish; this is the place where I have best fortune."

"And what sort of little fish do you catch here, O Hymir?" asked Thor.

"Whales!" answered the giant proudly. "I fish for nothing smaller than whales."

"Pooh!" cried Thor. "Who would fish for such small fry! Whales, indeed; let us row out further, where we can find something really worth catching," and he began to pull even faster than before.

"Stop! stop!" roared the giant. "You do not know what you are doing. These are the haunts of the dreadful Midgard serpent, and it is not safe to fish in these waters."

"Oho! The Midgard serpent!" said Thor, delighted. "That is the very fish I am after. Let us drop in our lines here."

Thor baited his great hook with the whole head of the ox which he had brought, and cast his line, big round as a man's arm, over the side of the boat. Hymir also cast his line, for he did not wish Thor to think him a coward; but his hand trembled as he waited for a bite, and he glanced down into the blue depths with eyes rounded as big as dinner-plates through fear of the horrible creature who lived down below those waves.

"Look! You have a bite!" cried Thor, so suddenly that Hymir started and nearly tumbled out of the boat. Hand over hand he pulled in his line, and lo! he had caught two whales—two great flopping whales—on his one hook! That was a catch indeed.

Hymir smiled proudly, forgetting his fear as he said, "How is that, my friend? Let us see you beat this catch in your morning's fishing."

Lo, just at that moment Thor also had a bite—such a bite! The boat rocked to and fro, and seemed ready to capsize every minute. Then the waves began to roll high and to be lashed into foam for yards and yards about the boat, as if some huge creature were struggling hard below the water.

"I have him!" shouted Thor; "I have the old serpent, the brother of the Fenris wolf! Pull, pull, monster! But you shall not escape me now!"

Sure enough, the Midgard serpent had Thor's hook fixed in his jaw, and struggle as he might, there was no freeing himself from the line; for the harder he pulled the stronger grew Thor. In his Æsir-might Thor waxed so huge and so forceful that his legs went straight through the bottom of the boat and his feet stood on the bottom of the sea. With firm bottom as a brace for his strength, Thor pulled and pulled, and at last up came the head of the Midgard serpent, up to the side of the boat, where it thrust out of the water mountain high, dreadful to behold; his monstrous red eyes were rolling fiercely, his nostrils spouted fire, and from his terrible sharp teeth dripped poison, that sizzled as it fell into the sea. Angrily they glared at each other, Thor and the serpent, while the water streamed into the boat, and the giant turned pale with fear at the danger threatening him on all sides.

Thor seized his hammer, preparing to smite the creature's head; but even as he swung Miölnir high for the fatal blow, Hymir cut the fish-line with his knife, and down into the depths of ocean sank the Midgard serpent amid a whirlpool of eddies. But the hammer had sped from Thor's iron fingers. It crushed the serpent's head as he sank downward to his lair on the sandy bottom; it crushed, but did not kill him, thanks to the giant's treachery. Terrible was the disturbance it caused beneath the waves. It burst the rocks and made the caverns of the ocean shiver into bits. It wrecked the coral groves and tore loose the draperies of sea-weed. The fishes scurried about in every direction, and the sea-monsters wildly sought new places to hide themselves when they found their homes destroyed. The sea itself was stirred to its lowest depths, and the waves ran trembling into one another's arms. The earth, too, shrank and shivered. Hymir, cowering low in the boat, was glad of one thing, which was that the terrible Midgard serpent had vanished out of sight. And that was the last that was ever seen of him, though he still lived, wounded and sore from the shock of Thor's hammer.

Now it was time to return home. Silently and sulkily the giant swam back to land; Thor, bearing the boat upon his shoulders, filled with water and weighted as it was with the great whales which Hymir had caught, waded ashore, and brought his burden to the giant's hall. Here Hymir met him crossly enough, for he was ashamed of the whole morning's work, in which Thor had appeared so much more of a hero than he. Indeed, he was tired of even pretending hospitality towards this unwelcome guest, and was resolved to be rid of him; but first he would put Thor to shame.

"You are a strong fellow," he said, "good at the oar and at the fishing; most wondrously good at the hammer, by which I know that you are Thor. But there is one thing which you cannot do, I warrant,—you cannot break this little cup of mine, hard though you may try."

"That I shall see for myself," answered Thor; and he took the cup in his hand. Now this was a magic cup, and there was but one way of breaking it, but one thing hard enough to shatter its mightiness. Thor threw it with all his force against a stone of the flooring; but instead of breaking the cup, the stone itself was cracked into splinters. Then Thor grew angry, for the giant and all his servants were laughing as if this were the greatest joke ever played.

"Ho, ho! Try again, Thor!" cried Hymir, nearly bursting with delight; for he thought that now he should prove how much mightier he was than the visitor from Asgard. Thor clutched the cup more firmly and hurled it against one of the iron pillars of the hall; but like a rubber ball the magic cup merely bounded back straight into Hymir's hand. At this second failure the giants were full of merriment and danced about, making all manner of fun at the expense of Thor. You can fancy how well Thor the mighty enjoyed this! His brow grew black, and the glance of his eye was terrible. He knew there was some magic in the trick, but he knew not how to meet it. Just then he felt the soft touch of a woman's hand upon his arm, and the voice of Týr's mother whispered in his ear,—

"Cast the cup against Hymir's own forehead, which is the hardest substance in the world." No one except Thor heard the woman say these words, for all the giant folk were doubled up with mirth over their famous joke. But Thor dropped upon one knee, and seizing the cup fiercely, whirled it about his head, then dashed it with all his might straight at Hymir's forehead. Smash! Crash! What had happened? Thor looked eagerly to see. There stood the giant, looking surprised and a little dazed; but his forehead showed not even a scratch, while the strong cup was shivered into little pieces.

"Well done!" exclaimed Hymir hastily, when he had recovered a little from his surprise. But he was mortified at Thor's success, and set about to think up a new task to try his strength. "That was very well," he remarked patronizingly; "now you must perform a harder task. Let us see you carry the mead kettle out of the hall. Do that, my fine fellow, and I shall say you are strong indeed."

The mead kettle! The very thing Thor had come to get! He glanced at Týr; he shot a look at Týr's mother; and both of them caught the sparkle, which was very like a wink. To himself Thor muttered, "I must not fail in this! I must not, will not fail!"

"First let me try," cried Tŷr; for he wanted to give Thor time for a resting-spell. Twice Tŷr the mighty strained at the great kettle, but he could not so much as stir one leg of it from the floor where it rested. He tugged and heaved in vain, growing red in the face, till his mother begged him to give over, for it was quite useless.

Then Thor stepped forth upon the floor. He grasped the rim of the kettle, and stamped his feet through the stone of the flooring as he braced himself to lift. One, two, three! Thor straightened himself, and up swung the giant kettle to his head, while the iron handle clattered about his feet. It was a mighty burden, and Thor staggered as he started for the door; but Tŷr was close beside him, and they had covered long leagues of ground on their way home before the astonished giants had recovered sufficiently to follow them. When Thor and Tŷr looked back, however, they saw a vast crowd of horrible giants, some of them with a hundred heads, swarming out of the caverns in Hymir's land, howling and prowling upon their track.

"You must stop them, Thor, or they will never let us get away with their precious kettle,—they take such long strides!" cried Tŷr. So Thor set down the kettle, and from his pocket drew out Miölnir, his wondrous hammer. Terribly it flashed in the air as he swung it over his head; then forth it flew towards Jotunheim; and before it returned to Thor's hand it had crushed all the heads of those many-headed giants, Hymir's ugly mother and Hymir himself among them. The only one who escaped was the good and beautiful mother of Tŷr. And you may be sure she lived happily ever after in the palace which Hymir and his wicked old mother had formerly made so wretched a home for her.

Now Tŷr and Thor had the giant kettle which they had gone so far and had met so many dangers to obtain. They took it to Œgir's sea-palace, where the banquet was still going on, and where the Æsir were still waiting patiently for their mead; for time does not go so fast below the

quiet waves as on shore. Now that King Œgir had the
great kettle, he could brew all the mead they needed. So
every one thanked Týr and congratulated Thor upon the
success of their adventure.

"I was sure that Thor would bring the kettle," said fair
Sif, smiling upon her brave husband.

"What Thor sets out to do, that he always accom-
plishes," said Father Odin gravely. And that was praise
enough for any one.

Thor's Duel

In the days that are past a wonderful race of horses pastured in the meadows of heaven, steeds more beautiful and more swift than any which the world knows to-day. There was Hrîmfaxi, the black, sleek horse who drew the chariot of Night across the sky and scattered the dew from his foaming bit. There was Glad, behind whose flying heels sped the swift chariot of Day. His mane was yellow with gold, and from it beamed light which made the whole world bright. Then there were the two shining horses of the sun, Arvakur the watchful, and Alsvith the rapid; and the nine fierce battle-chargers of the nine Valkyries, who bore the bodies of fallen heroes from the field of fight to the blessedness of Valhalla. Each of the gods had his own glorious steed, with such pretty names as Gold-mane and Silver-top, Light-foot and Precious-stone; these galloped with their masters over clouds and through the blue air, blowing flame from their nostrils and glinting sparks from their fiery eyes. The Æsir would have been poor indeed without their faithful mounts, and few would be the stories to tell in which these noble creatures do not bear at least a part.

But best of all the horses of heaven was Sleipnir, the eight-legged steed of Father Odin, who because he was so well supplied with sturdy feet could gallop faster over land and sea than any horse which ever lived. Sleipnir was snow-white and beautiful to see, and Odin was very fond and proud of him, you may be sure. He loved to ride forth upon his good horse's back to meet whatever adventure might be upon the way, and sometimes they had wild times together.

One day Odin galloped off from Asgard upon Sleipnir straight towards Jotunheim and the Land of Giants, for it was long since All-Father had been to the cold country, and he wished to see how its mountains and ice-rivers looked. Now as he galloped along a wild road, he met a huge giant standing beside his giant steed.

"Who goes there?" cried the giant gruffly, blocking the way so that Odin could not pass. "You with the golden helmet, who are you, who ride so famously through air and water? For I have been watching you from this mountain-top. Truly, that is a fine horse which you bestride."

"There is no finer horse in all the world," boasted Odin. "Have you not heard of Sleipnir, the pride of Asgard? I will match him against any of your big, clumsy giant horses."

"Ho!" roared the giant angrily, "an excellent horse he is, your little Sleipnir. But I warrant he is no match for my Gullfaxi here. Come, let us try a race; and at its end I shall pay you for your insult to our horses of Jotunheim."

So saying, the giant, whose ugly name was Hrungnir, sprang upon his horse and spurred straight at Odin in the narrow way. Odin turned and galloped back towards Asgard with all his might; for not only must he prove his horse's speed, but he must save himself and Sleipnir from the anger of the giant, who was one of the fiercest and wickedest of all his fierce and wicked race.

How the eight slender legs of Sleipnir twinkled through the blue sky! How his nostrils quivered and shot forth fire and smoke! Like a flash of lightning he darted across the sky, and the giant horse rumbled and thumped along close behind like the thunder following the flash.

"Hi, hi!" yelled the giant. "After them, Gullfaxi! And when we have overtaken the two, we will crush their bones between us!"

"Speed, speed, my Sleipnir!" shouted Odin. "Speed, good horse, or you will never again feed in the dewy pastures of Asgard with the other horses. Speed, speed, and bring us safe within the gates!"

Well Sleipnir understood what his master said, and well he knew the way. Already the rainbow bridge was in sight, with Heimdal the watchman prepared to let them in. His sharp eyes had spied them afar, and had recognized the flash of Sleipnir's white body and of Odin's golden helmet. Gallop and thud! The twelve hoofs were upon the bridge, the giant horse close behind the other. At last Hrungnir knew where he was, and into what danger he was rushing. He pulled at the reins and tried to stop his great beast. But Gullfaxi was tearing along at too terrible a speed. He could not stop. Heimdal threw open the gates of Asgard, and in galloped Sleipnir with his precious burden, safe. Close upon them bolted in Gullfaxi, bearing his giant master, puffing and purple in the face from hard riding and anger. Cling-clang! Heimdal had shut and barred the gates, and there was the giant prisoned in the castle of his enemies.

Now the Æsir were courteous folk, unlike the giants, and they were not anxious to take advantage of a single enemy thus thrown into their power. They invited him to enter Valhalla with them, to rest and sup before the long journey of his return. Thor was not present, so they filled for the giant the great cups which Thor was wont to drain, for they were nearest to the giant size. But you remember that Thor was famous for his power to drink deep. Hrungnir's head was not so steady; Thor's draught was too much for him. He soon lost his wits, of which he had but few; and a witless giant is a most dreadful creature. He raged like a madman, and threatened to pick up Valhalla like a toy house and carry it home with him to Jotunheim. He said he would pull Asgard to pieces and slay all the gods except Freia the fair and Sif, the golden-haired wife of Thor, whom he would carry off like little dolls for his toy house.

The Æsir knew not what to do, for Thor and his hammer were not there to protect them, and Asgard seemed in danger with this enemy within its very walls. Hrungnir called for more and more mead, which Freia alone dared to bring and set before him. And the more he drank the fiercer he became. At last the Æsir could bear no longer his insults and his violence. Besides, they feared that there would be no more mead left for their banquets if this unwelcome visitor should keep Freia pouring out for him Thor's mighty goblets. They bade Heimdal blow his horn and summon Thor; and this Heimdal did in a trice.

Now rumbling and thundering in his chariot of goats came Thor. He dashed into the hall, hammer in hand, and stared in amazement at the unwieldy guest whom he found there.

"A giant feasting in Asgard hall!" he roared. "This is a sight which I never saw before. Who gave the insolent fellow leave to sit in my place? And why does fair Freia wait upon him as if he were some noble guest at a feast of the high gods? I will slay him at once!" and he raised the hammer to keep his word.

Thor's coming had sobered the giant somewhat, for he knew that this was no enemy to be trifled with. He looked at Thor sulkily and said: "I am Odin's guest. He invited me to this banquet, and therefore I am under his protection."

"You shall be sorry that you accepted the invitation," cried Thor, balancing his hammer and looking very fierce; for Sif had sobbed in his ear how the giant had threatened to carry her away.

Hrungnir now rose to his feet and faced Thor boldly, for the sound of Thor's gruff voice had restored his scattered wits. "I am here alone and without weapons," he said. "You would do ill to slay me now. It would be little like the noble Thor, of whom we hear tales, to do such a thing. The world will count you braver if you let me go and meet me later in single combat, when we shall both be fairly armed."

Thor dropped the hammer to his side. "Your words are true," he said, for he was a just and honorable fellow.

"I was foolish to leave my shield and stone club at home," went on the giant. "If I had my arms with me, we would fight at this moment. But I name you a coward if you slay me now, an unarmed enemy."

"Your words are just," quoth Thor again. "I have never before been challenged by any foe. I will meet you, Hrungnir, at your Stone City, midway between heaven and earth. And there we will fight a duel to see which of us is the better fellow."

Hrungnir departed for Stone City in Jotunheim; and great was the excitement of the other giants when they heard of the duel which one of their number was to fight with Thor, the deadliest enemy of their race.

"We must be sure that Hrungnir wins the victory!" they cried. "It will never do to have Asgard victorious in the first duel that we have fought with her champion. We will make a second hero to aid Hrungnir."

All the giants set to work with a will. They brought great buckets of moist clay, and heaping them up into a huge mound, moulded the mass with their giant hands as a sculptor does his image, until they had made a man of clay, an immense dummy, nine miles high and three miles wide. "Now we must make him live; we must put a heart into him!" they cried. But they could find no heart big enough until they thought of taking that of a mare, and that fitted nicely. A mare's heart is the most cowardly one that beats.

Hrungnir's heart was a three-cornered piece of hard stone. His head also was of stone, and likewise the great shield which he held before him when he stood outside of Stone City waiting for Thor to come to the duel. Over his shoulder he carried his club, and that also was of stone, the kind from which whetstones are made, hard and terrible. By his side stood the huge clay man, Möckuralfi, and they were a dreadful sight to see, these two vast bodies whom Thor must encounter.

But at the very first sight of Thor, who came thundering

to the place with swift Thialfi his servant, the timid mare's heart in the man of clay throbbed with fear; he trembled so that his knees knocked together, and his nine miles of height rocked unsteadily.

Thialfi ran up to Hrungnir and began to mock him, saying, "You are careless, giant. I fear you do not know what a mighty enemy has come to fight you. You hold your shield in front of you; but that will serve you nothing. Thor has seen this. He has only to go down into the earth and he can attack you conveniently from beneath your very feet."

At this terrifying news Hrungnir hastened to throw his shield upon the ground and to stand upon it, so that he might be safe from Thor's under-stroke. He grasped his heavy club with both hands and waited. He had not long to wait. There came a blinding flash of lightning and a peal of crashing thunder. Thor had cast his hammer into space. Hrungnir raised his club with both hands and hurled it against the hammer which he saw flying towards him. The two mighty weapons met in the air with an ear-splitting shock. Hard as was the stone of the giant's club, it was like glass against the power of Miölnir. The club was dashed into pieces; some fragments fell upon the earth; and these, they say, are the rocks from which whetstones are made unto this day. They are so hard that men use them to sharpen knives and axes and scythes. One splinter of the hard stone struck Thor himself in the forehead, with so fierce a blow that he fell forward upon the ground, and Thialfi feared that he was killed. But Miölnir, not even stopped in its course by meeting the giant's club, sped straight to Hrungnir and crushed his stony skull, so that he fell forward over Thor, and his foot lay on the fallen hero's neck. And that was the end of the giant whose head and heart were of stone.

Meanwhile Thialfi the swift had fought with the man of clay, and had found little trouble in toppling him to earth. For the mare's cowardly heart in his great body gave him little strength to meet Thor's faithful servant; and the trembling limbs of Möckuralfi soon yielded to Thialfi's hearty blows. He fell like an unsteady tower of blocks, and his brittle bulk shivered into a thousand fragments. Thialfi ran to his master and tried to raise him. The giant's great foot still rested upon his neck, and all Thialfi's strength could not move it away. Swift as the wind he ran for the other Æsir, and when they heard that great Thor, their champion, had fallen and seemed like one dead, they came rushing to the spot in horror and confusion. Together they all attempted to raise Hrungnir's foot from Thor's neck that they might see whether their hero lived or no. But all their efforts were in vain. The foot was not to be lifted by Æsir-might.

At this moment a second hero appeared upon the scene. It was Magni, the son of Thor himself; Magni, who was but three days old, yet already in his babyhood he was almost as big as a giant and had nearly the strength of his father. This wonderful youngster came running to the place where his father lay surrounded by a group of sad-faced and despairing gods. When Magni saw what the matter was, he seized Hrungnir's enormous foot in both his hands, heaved his broad young shoulders, and in a moment Thor's neck was free of the weight which was crushing it.

Best of all, it proved that Thor was not dead, only stunned by the blow of the giant's club and by his fall. He stirred, sat up painfully, and looked around him at the group of eager friends. "Who lifted the weight from my neck?" he asked.

"It was I, father," answered Magni modestly. Thor clasped him in his arms and hugged him tight, beaming with pride and gratitude.

"Truly, you are a fine child!" he cried; "one to make glad your father's heart. Now as a reward for your first great deed you shall have a gift from me. The swift horse of Hrungnir shall be yours,—that same Gullfaxi who was the

beginning of all this trouble. You shall ride Gullfaxi; only a
giant steed is strong enough to bear the weight of such an
infant prodigy as you, my Magni. "

Now this word did not wholly please Father Odin, for he
thought that a horse so excellent ought to belong to him.
He took Thor aside and argued that but for him there
would have been no duel, no horse to win. Thor answered
simply,—

"True, Father Odin, you began this trouble. But I have
fought your battle, destroyed your enemy, and suffered
great pain for you. Surely, I have won the horse fairly and
may give it to whom I choose. My son, who has saved me,
deserves a horse as good as any. Yet, as you have proved,
even Gullfaxi is scarce a match for your Sleipnir. Verily,
Father Odin, you should be content with the best." Odin
said no more.

Now Thor went home to his cloud-palace in Thrudvang.
And there he was healed of all his hurts except that which
the splinter of stone had made in his forehead. For the
stone was imbedded so fast that it could not be taken out,
and Thor suffered sorely therefor. Sif, his yellow-haired
wife, was in despair, knowing not what to do. At last she
bethought her of the wise woman, Groa, who had skill in
all manner of herbs and witch-charms. Sif sent for Groa,
who lived all alone and sad because her husband
Örvandil had disappeared, she knew not whither. Groa
came to Thor and, standing beside his bed while he slept,
sang strange songs and gently waved her hands over him.
Immediately the stone in his forehead began to loosen,
and Thor opened his eyes.

"The stone is loosening, the stone is coming out!" he
cried. "How can I reward you, gentle dame? Prithee, what
is your name?"

"My name is Groa," answered the woman, weeping,
"wife of Örvandil who is lost."

"Now, then, I can reward you, kind Groa!" cried Thor,
"for I can bring you tidings of your husband. I met him in
the cold country, in Jotunheim, the Land of Giants, which

you know I sometimes visit for a bit of good hunting. It was by Elivâgar's icy river that I met Örvandil, and there was no way for him to cross. So I put him in an iron basket and myself bore him over the flood. Br-r-r! But that is a cold land! His feet stuck out through the meshes of the basket, and when we reached the other side one of his toes was frozen stiff. So I broke it off and tossed it up into the sky that it might become a star. To prove that what I relate is true, Groa, there is the new star shining over us at this very moment. Look! From this day it shall be known to men as Örvandil's Toe. Do not you weep any longer. After all, the loss of a toe is a little thing; and I promise that your husband shall soon return to you, safe and sound, but for that small token of his wanderings in the land where visitors are not welcome."

At these joyful tidings poor Groa was so overcome that she fainted. And that put an end to the charm which she was weaving to loosen the stone from Thor's forehead. The stone was not yet wholly free, and thenceforth it was in vain to attempt its removal; Thor must always wear the splinter in his forehead. Groa could never forgive herself for the carelessness which had thus made her skill vain to help one to whom she had reason to be so grateful.

Now because of the bit of whetstone in Thor's forehead, folk of olden times were very careful how they used a whetstone; and especially they knew that they must not throw or drop one on the floor. For when they did so, the splinter in Thor's forehead was jarred, and the good Asa suffered great pain.

In the Giant's House

Although Thor had slain Thiasse the giant builder, Thrym the thief, Hrungnir, and Hymir, and had rid the world of whole families of wicked giants, there remained many others in Jotunheim to do their evil deeds and to plot mischief against both gods and men; and of these Geirröd was the fiercest and the wickedest. He and his two ugly daughters—Gialp of the red eyes, and Greip of the black teeth—lived in a large palace among the mountains, where Geirröd had his treasures of iron and copper, silver and gold; for, since the death of Thrym, Geirröd was the Lord of the Mines, and all the riches that came out of the earth-caverns belonged to him.

Thrym had been Geirröd's friend, and the tale of Thrym's death through the might of Thor and his hammer had made Geirröd very sad and angry. "If I could but catch Thor, now, without his weapons," he said to his daughters, "what a lesson I would give him! How I would punish him for his deeds against us giants!"

"Oh, what would you do, father?" cried Gialp, twinkling her cruel red eyes, and working her claw fingers as if she would like to fasten them in Thor's golden beard.

"Oh, what would you do, father?" cried Greip, smacking her lips and grinding her black teeth as if she would like a bite out of Thor's stout arm.

"Do to him!" growled Geirröd fiercely. "Do to him! Gr-r-r! I would chew him all up! I would break his bones into little bits! I would smash him into jelly!"

"Oh, good, good! Do it, father, and then give him to us to play with," cried Gialp and Greip, dancing up and down till the hills trembled and all the frightened sheep ran home to their folds thinking that there must be an earthquake; for Gialp was as tall as a pine-tree and many times as thick, while Greip, her little sister, was as large around as a haystack and high as a flagstaff. They both hoped some day to be as huge as their father, whose legs were so long that he could step across the river valleys from one hilltop to another, just as we human folk cross a brook on stepping-stones; and his arms were so stout that he could lift a yoke of oxen in each fist, as if they were red-painted toys.

Geirröd shook his head at his two playful daughters and sighed. "We must catch Master Thor first, my girls, before we do these fine things to him. We must catch him without his mighty hammer, that never fails him, and without his belt, that doubles his strength whenever he puts it on, or even I cannot chew and break and smash him as he deserves; for with these his weapons he is the mightiest creature in the whole world, and I would rather meddle with thunder and lightning than with him. Let us wait, children."

Then Gialp and Greip pouted and sulked like two great babies who cannot have the new plaything which they want; and very ugly they were to see, with tears as big as oranges rolling down their cheeks.

Sooner than they expected they came very near to having their heart's desire fulfilled. And if it had happened as they wished, and if Asgard had lost its goodliest hero, its strongest defense, that would have been red Loki's fault, all Loki's evil planning; for you are now to hear of the wickedest thing that up to this time Loki had ever done. As you know, it was Loki who was Thor's bitterest enemy; and for many months he had been awaiting the chance to repay the Thunder Lord for the dole which Thor had brought upon him at the time of the dwarf's gifts to Asgard.

This is how it came about: Loki had long remembered the fun of skimming as a great bird in Freia's falcon feathers. He had longed to borrow the wings once again and to fly away over the round world to see what he could see; for he thought that so he could learn many secrets which he was not meant to know, and plan wonderful mischief without being found out. But Freia would not again loan her feather dress to Loki. She owed him a grudge for naming her as Thrym's bride; and besides, she remembered his treatment of Idun, and she did not trust his oily tongue and fine promises. So Loki saw no way but to borrow the feathers without leave; and this he did one day when Freia was gone to ride in her chariot drawn by white cats. Loki put on the feather dress, as he had done twice before,— once when he went to Jotunheim to bring back stolen Idun and her magic apples, once when he went to find out about Thor's hammer.

Away he flew from Asgard as birdlike as you please, chuckling to himself with wicked thoughts. It did not make any particular difference to him where he went. It was such fun to flap and fly, skim and wheel, looking and feeling for all the world like a big brown falcon. He swooped low, thinking, "I wonder what Freia would say to see me now! Whee-e-e! How angry she would be!" Just then he spied the high wall of a palace on the mountains.

"Oho!" said Loki. "I never saw that place before. It may be a giant's dwelling. I think this must be Jotunheim, from the bigness of things. I must just peep to see." Loki was the most inquisitive of creatures, as wily minded folk are apt to be.

Loki the falcon alighted and hopped to the wall, then giving a flap of his wings he flew up and up to the window ledge, where he perched and peered into the hall. And there within he saw the giant Geirröd with his daughters eating their dinner. They looked so ugly and so greedy, as they sat there gobbling their food in giant mouthfuls, that

Loki on the window-sill could not help snickering to himself. Now at that sound Geirröd looked up and saw the big brown bird peeping in at the window. "Heigha!" cried the giant to one of his servants. "Go you and fetch me the big brown bird up yonder in the window."

Then the servant ran to the wall and tried to climb up to get at Loki; but the window was so high that he could not reach. He jumped and slipped, scrambled and slipped, again and again, while Loki sat just above his clutching fingers, and chuckled so that he nearly fell from his perch. "Te-he! te-he!" chattered Loki in the falcon tongue. It was such fun to see the fellow grow black in the face with trying to reach him that Loki thought he would wait until the giant's fingers almost touched him, before flying away.

But Loki waited too long. At last, with a quick spring, the giant gained a hold upon the window ledge, and Loki was within reach. When Loki flapped his wings to fly, he found that his feet were tangled in the vine that grew upon the wall. He struggled and twisted with all his might,—but in vain. There he was, caught fast. Then the servant grasped him by the legs, and so brought him to Geirröd, where he sat at table. Now Loki in his feather dress looked exactly like a falcon—except for his eyes. There was no hiding the wise and crafty look of Loki's eyes. As soon as Geirröd looked at him, he suspected that this was no ordinary bird.

"You are no falcon, you!" he cried. "You are spying about my palace in disguise. Speak, and tell me who you are." Loki was afraid to tell, because he knew the giants were angry with him for his part in Thrym's death,—small though his part had really been in that great deed. So he kept his beak closed tight, and refused to speak. The giant stormed and raged and threatened to kill him; but still Loki was silent.

Then Geirröd locked the falcon up in a chest for three long months without food or water, to see how that would

suit his birdship. You can imagine how hungry and thirsty
Loki was at the end of that time,—ready to tell anything
he knew, and more also, for the sake of a crumb of bread
and a drop of water.

So then Geirröd called through the keyhole, "Well, Sir
Falcon, now will you tell me who you are?" And this time
Loki piped feebly, "I am Loki of Asgard; give me something
to eat!"

"Oho!" quoth the giant fiercely. "You are that Loki who
went with Thor to kill my brother Thrym! Oho! Well, you
shall die for that, my feathered friend!"

"No, no!" screamed Loki. "Thor is no friend of mine. I
love the giants far better! One of them is my wife!"—which
was indeed true, as were few of Loki's words.

"Then if Thor is no friend of yours, to save your life will
you bring him into my power?" asked Geirröd.

Loki's eyes gleamed wickedly among the feathers. Here
all at once was his chance to be free, and to have his
revenge upon Thor, his worst enemy. "Ay, that I will!" he
cried eagerly. "I will bring Thor into your power."

So Geirröd made him give a solemn promise to do that
wrong; and upon this he loosed Loki from the chest and
gave him food. Then they formed the wicked plan
together, while Gialp and Greip, the giant's ugly daughters, listened and smacked their lips.

Loki was to persuade Thor to come with him to
Geirrödsgard. More; he must come without his mighty
hammer, and without the iron gloves of power, and without the belt of strength; for so only could the giant have
Thor at his mercy.

After their wicked plans were made, Loki bade a
friendly farewell to Geirröd and his daughters and flew
back to Asgard as quickly as he could. You may be sure he
had a sound scolding from Freia for stealing her feather
dress and for keeping it so long. But he told such a pitiful
story of being kept prisoner by a cruel giant, and he
looked in truth so pale and thin from his long fast, that the
gods were fain to pity him and to believe his story, in spite

of the many times that he had deceived them. Indeed, most of his tale was true, but he told only half of the truth; for he spoke no word of his promise to the giant. This he kept hidden in his breast.

Now, one day not long after this, Loki invited Thor to go on a journey with him to visit a new friend who, he said, was anxious to know the Thunder Lord. Loki was so pleasant in his manner and seemed so frank in his speech that Thor, whose heart was simple and unsuspicious, never dreamed of any wrong, not even when Loki added,—"And by the bye, my Thor, you must leave behind your hammer, your belt, and your gloves; for it would show little courtesy to wear such weapons in the home of a new friend."

Thor carelessly agreed; for he was pleased with the idea of a new adventure, and with the thought of making a new friend. Besides, on their last journey together, Loki had behaved so well that Thor believed him to have changed his evil ways and to have become his friend. So together they set off in Thor's goat chariot, without weapons of any kind except those which Loki secretly carried. Loki chuckled as they rattled over the clouds, and if Thor had seen the look in his eyes, he would have turned the chariot back to Asgard and to safety, where he had left gentle Sif his wife. But Thor did not notice, and so they rumbled on.

Soon they came to the gate of Giant Land. Thor thought this strange, for he knew they were like to find few friends of his dwelling among the Big Folk. For the first time he began to suspect Loki of some treacherous scheme. However, he said nothing, and pretended to be as gay and careless as before. But he thought of a plan to find out the truth.

Close by the entrance was the cave of Grid, a good giantess, who alone of all her race was a friend of Thor and of the folk in Asgard.

"I will alight here for a moment, Loki," said Thor carelessly. "I long for a draught of water. Hold you the goats tightly by the reins until I return."

So he went into the cave and got his draught of water. But while he was drinking, he questioned good mother Grid to some purpose.

"Who is this friend Geirröd whom I go to see?" he asked her.

"Geirröd your friend! You go to see Geirröd!" she exclaimed. He is the wickedest giant of us all, and no friend to you. Why do you go, dear Thor?"

"H'm!" muttered Thor. "Red Loki's mischief again!" He told her of the visit that Loki had proposed, and how he had left at home the belt, the gloves, and the hammer which made him stronger than any giant. Then Grid was frightened.

"Go not, go not, Thor!" she begged. Geirröd will kill you, and those ugly girls, Gialp and Greip, will have the pleasure of crunching your bones. Oh, I know them well, the hussies!"

But Thor declared that he would go, whether or no. "I have promised Loki that I will go," he said, "and go I will; for I always keep my word."

"Then you shall have three little gifts of me," quoth she. "Here is my belt of power—for I also have one like your own." And she buckled about his waist a great belt, at whose touch he felt his strength redoubled. "This is my iron glove," she said, as she put one on his mighty hand, "and with it, as with your own, you can handle lightning and touch unharmed the hottest of red-hot metal. And here, last of all," she added, "is Gridarvöll, my good staff, which you may find useful. Take them, all three; and may Sif see you safe at home again by their aid."

Thor thanked her and went out once more to join Loki, who never suspected what had happened in the cave. For the belt and the glove were hidden under Thor's cloak. And as for the staff, it was quite ordinary looking, as if Thor might have picked it up anywhere along the road.

On they journeyed until they came to the river Vimer, the greatest of all rivers, which roared and tossed in a terrible way between them and the shore which they wanted to reach. It seemed impossible to cross. But Thor drew his belt a little tighter, and planting Grid's staff firmly on the bottom, stepped out into the stream. Loki clung behind to his cloak, frightened out of his wits. But Thor waded on bravely, his strength doubled by Grid's belt, and his steps supported by her magic staff. Higher and higher the waves washed over his knees, his waist, his shoulders, as if they were fierce to drown him. And Thor said,—

"Ho there, river Vimer! Do not grow any larger, I pray. It is of no use. The more you crowd upon me, the mightier I grow with my belt and my staff!"

But lo! as he nearly reached the other side, Thor spied some one hiding close down by the bank of the river. It was Gialp of the red eyes, the big elder daughter of Geirröd. She was splashing the water upon Thor, making the great waves that rolled up and threatened to drown him.

"Oho!" cried he. "So it is you who are making the river rise, big little girl. We must see to that"; and seizing a huge boulder, he hurled it at her. It hit her with a thud, for Thor's aim never missed. Giving a scream as loud as a steam-whistle, Gialp limped home as best she could to tell her father, and to prepare a warm reception for the stranger who bore Loki at his back.

When Thor had pulled himself out of the river by some bushes, he soon came to the palace which Loki had first sighted in his falcon dress. And there he found everything most courteously made ready for him. He and Loki were received like dear old friends, with shouts of rejoicing and ringing of bells. Geirröd himself came out to meet them, and would have embraced his new friend Thor; but the Thunder Lord merely seized him by the hand and gave him so hearty a squeeze with the iron glove that the giant howled with pain. Yet he could say nothing, for Thor looked pleased and gentle. And Geirröd said to himself, "Ho, ho, my fine little Thor! I will soon pay you for that handshake, and for many things beside."

All this time Gialp and Greip did not appear, and Loki also had taken himself away, to be out of danger when the

hour of Thor's death should come. For he feared that
dreadful things might happen before Thor died; and he
did not want to be remembered by the big fist of the com-
panion whom he had betrayed. Loki, having kept his
promise to the giant, was even now far on the road back
to Asgard, where he meant with a sad face to tell the gods
that Thor had been slain by a horrible giant; but never to
tell them how.

So Thor was all alone when the servants led him to the
chamber which Geirröd had made ready for his dear
friend. It was a wonderfully fine chamber, to be sure; but
the strange thing about it was that among the furnishings
there was but one chair, a giant chair, with a drapery all
about the legs. Now Thor was very weary with his long
journey, and he sat down in the chair to rest. Then, wonderful to tell!—if elevators had been invented in those
days, he might have thought he was in one. For instantly
the seat of the chair shot up towards the roof, and against
this he was in danger of being crushed as Geirröd had
longed to see him. But quick as a flash Thor raised the
staff which good old Grid had given him, and pushed it
against the rafters with all his might to stop his upward
journey. It was a tremendous push that he gave.
Something cracked; something crashed; the chair fell to
the ground as Thor leaped off the seat, and there were
two terrible screams.

Then Thor found—what do you think? Why, that Gialp
and Greip, the giant's daughters, had hidden under the
seat of the chair, and had lifted it up on their backs to
crush Thor against the roof! But instead of that, it was
Thor who had broken their backs, so that they lay dead
upon the floor like limp rag dolls.

Now this little exercise had only given Thor an excellent
appetite for supper. So that when word came bidding him
to the banquet, he was very glad.

"First," said big Geirröd, grinning horribly, for he did
not know what had happened to his daughters,—"first we
will see some games, friend Thor."

Then Thor came into the hall, where fires were burning
in great chimney places along the walls. "It is here that we
play our little games," cried Geirröd. And on the moment,
seizing a pair of tongs, he snatched a red-hot wedge of
iron from one of the fires and hurled it straight at Thor's
head. But Thor was quicker than he. Swift as a flash he
caught the flying spark in his iron glove, and calling forth
all the might of Grid's belt, he cast the wedge back at the
giant. Geirröd dodged behind an iron pillar, but it was in
vain. Thor's might was such as no iron could meet. Like a
bolt of lightning the wedge passed through the pillar,
through Geirröd himself, through the thick wall of the
palace, and buried itself deep in the ground, where it
lodges to this day, unless some one has dug it up to sell
for old iron.

So perished Geirröd and his children, one of the
wickedest families of giants that ever lived in Jotunheim.
And so Thor escaped from the snares of Loki, who had
never done deed worse than this.

When Thor returned home to Asgard, where from Loki's
lying tale he found all the gods mourning him as dead, you
can fancy what a joyful reception he had. But for Loki, the
false-hearted, false-tongued traitor to them all, there was
only hatred. He no longer had any friends among the good
folk. The wicked giants and the monsters of Utgard were
now his only friends, for he had grown to be like them,
and even these did not trust him overmuch.

Balder and the Mistletoe

Loki had given up trying to revenge himself upon Thor. The Thunder Lord seemed proof against his tricks. And indeed nowadays Loki hated him no more than he did the other gods. He hated some because they always frowned at him; he hated others because they only laughed and jeered. Some he hated for their distrust and some for their fear. But he hated them all because they were happy and good and mighty, while he was wretched, bad, and of little might. Yet it was all his own fault that this was so. He might have been an equal with the best of them, if he had not chosen to set himself against everything that was good. He had made them all his enemies, and the more he did to injure them, the more he hated them,—which is always the way with evil-doers. Loki longed to see them all unhappy. He slunk about in Asgard with a glum face and wrinkled forehead. He dared not meet the eyes of any one, lest they should read his heart. For he was plotting evil, the greatest of evils, which should bring sorrow to all his enemies at once and turn Asgard into a land of mourning. The Æsir did not guess the whole truth, yet they felt the bitterness of the thoughts which Loki bore; and whenever in the dark he passed unseen, the gods shuddered as if a breath of evil had blown upon them, and even the flowers drooped before his steps.

Now at this time Balder the beautiful had a strange dream. He dreamed that a cloud came before the sun, and all Asgard was dark. He waited for the cloud to drift away, and for the sun to smile again. But no; the sun was gone forever, he thought; and Balder awoke feeling very sad. The next night Balder had another dream. This time he dreamed that it was still dark as before; the flowers were withered and the gods were growing old; even Idun's magic apples could not make them young again. And all were weeping and wringing their hands as though some dreadful thing had happened. Balder awoke feeling strangely frightened, yet he said no word to Nanna his wife, for he did not want to trouble her.

When it came night again Balder slept and dreamed a third dream, a still more terrible one than the other two had been. He thought that in the dark, lonely world there was nothing but a sad voice, which cried, "The sun is gone! The spring is gone! Joy is gone! For Balder the beautiful is dead, dead, dead!"

This time Balder awoke with a cry, and Nanna asked him what was the matter. So he had to tell her of his dream, and he was sadly frightened; for in those days dreams were often sent to folk as messages, and what the gods dreamed usually came true. Nanna ran sobbing to Queen Frigg, who was Balder's mother, and told her all the dreadful dream, asking what could be done to prevent it from coming true.

Now Balder was Queen Frigg's dearest son. Thor was older and stronger, and more famous for his great deeds; but Frigg loved far better gold-haired Balder. And indeed he was the best-beloved of all the Æsir; for he was gentle, fair, and wise, and wherever he went folk grew happy and light-hearted at the very sight of him, just as we do when we first catch a glimpse of spring peeping over the hilltop into Winterland. So when Frigg heard of Balder's woeful dream, she was frightened almost out of her wits.

"He must not die! He shall not die!" she cried. "He is so dear to all the world, how could there be anything which would hurt him?"

And then a wonderful thought came to Frigg. "I will travel over the world and make all things promise not to injure my boy," she said. "Nothing shall pass my notice. I will get the word of everything."

So first she went to the gods themselves, gathered on Ida Plain for their morning exercise; and telling them of Balder's dream, she begged them to give the promise. Oh, what a shout arose when they heard her words!

"Hurt Balder!—our Balder! Not for the world, we promise! The dream is wrong,—there is nothing so cruel as to wish harm to Balder the beautiful!" they cried. But deep in their hearts they felt a secret fear which would linger until they should hear that all things had given their promise. What if harm were indeed to come to Balder! The thought was too dreadful.

Then Frigg went to see all the beasts who live in field or forest or rocky den. Willingly they gave their promise never to harm hair of gentle Balder. "For he is ever kind to us," they said, "and we love him as if he were one of ourselves. Not with claws or teeth or hoofs or horns will any beast hurt Balder."

Next Frigg spoke to the birds and fishes, reptiles and insects. And all—even the venomous serpents—cried that Balder was their friend, and that they would never do aught to hurt his dear body. "Not with beak or talon, bite or sting or poison fang, will one of us hurt Balder," they promised.

After doing this, the anxious mother traveled over the whole round world, step by step; and from all the things that are she got the same ready promise never to harm Balder the beautiful. All the trees and plants promised; all the stones and metals; earth, air, fire, and water; sun, snow, wind, and rain, and all diseases that men know,— each gave to Frigg the word of promise which she wanted. So at last, footsore and weary, she came back to Asgard with the joyful news that Balder must be safe, for that there was nothing in the world but had promised to be his harmless friend.

Each arrow overshot his head.
See page 132.

Then there was rejoicing in Asgard, as if the gods had won one of their great victories over the giants. The noble Æsir and the heroes who had died in battle upon the earth, and who had come to Valhalla to live happily ever after, gathered on Ida Plain to celebrate the love of all nature for Balder.

There they invented a famous game, which was to prove how safe he was from the bite of death. They stationed Balder in the midst of them, his face glowing like the sun with the bright light which ever shone from him. And as he stood there all unarmed and smiling, by turns they tried all sorts of weapons against him; they made as if to beat him with sticks, they stoned him with stones, they shot at him with arrows and hurled mighty spears straight at his heart.

It was a merry game, and a shout of laughter went up as each stone fell harmless at Balder's feet, each stick broke before it touched his shoulders, each arrow overshot his head, and each spear turned aside. For neither stone nor wood nor flinty arrow-point nor barb of iron would break the promise which each had given. Balder was safe with them, just as if he were bewitched. He remained unhurt among the missiles which whizzed about his head, and which piled up in a great heap around the charmed spot whereon he stood.

Now among the crowd that watched these games with such enthusiasm, there was one face that did not smile, one voice that did not rasp itself hoarse with cheering. Loki saw how every one and every thing loved Balder, and he was jealous. He was the only creature in all the world that hated Balder and wished for his death. Yet Balder had never done harm to him. But the wicked plan that Loki had been cherishing was almost ripe, and in this poison fruit was the seed of the greatest sorrow that Asgard had ever known.

While the others were enjoying their game of love, Loki stole away unperceived from Ida Plain, and with a wig of gray hair, a long gown, and a staff, disguised himself as an old woman. Then he hobbled down Asgard streets till he came to the palace of Queen Frigg, the mother of Balder.

"Good-day, my lady," quoth the old woman, in a cracked voice. "What is that noisy crowd doing yonder in the green meadow? I am so deafened by their shouts that I can hardly hear myself think."

"Who are you, good mother, that you have not heard?" said Queen Frigg in surprise. "They are shooting at my son Balder. They are proving the word which all things have given me,—the promise not to injure my dear son. And that promise will be kept."

The old crone pretended to be full of wonder. "So, now!" she cried. "Do you mean to say that *every single thing* in the whole world has promised not to hurt your son? I can scarce believe it; though, to be sure, he is as fine a fellow as I ever saw." Of course this flattery pleased Frigg.

"You say true, mother," she answered proudly, "he is a noble son. Yes, everything has promised,—that is, everything except one tiny little plant that is not worth mentioning."

The old woman's eyes twinkled wickedly. "And what is that foolish little plant, my dear?" she asked coaxingly.

"It is the mistletoe that grows in the meadow west of Valhalla. It was too young to promise, and too harmless to bother with," answered Frigg carelessly.

After this her questioner hobbled painfully away. But as soon as she was out of sight from the Queen's palace, she picked up the skirts of her gown and ran as fast as she could to the meadow west of Valhalla. And there sure enough, as Frigg had said, was a tiny sprig of mistletoe growing on a gnarled oak-tree. The false Loki took out a knife which she carried in some hidden pocket and cut off the mistletoe very carefully. Then she trimmed and shaped it so that it was like a little green arrow, pointed at one end, but very slender.

"Ho, ho!" chuckled the old woman. "So you are the only thing in all the world that is too young to make a promise, my little mistletoe. Well, young as you are, you must go on

an errand for me to-day. And maybe you shall bear a message of my love to Balder the beautiful."

Then she hobbled back to Ida Plain, where the merry
game was still going on around Balder. Loki quietly passed
unnoticed through the crowd, and came close to the
elbow of a big dark fellow who was standing lonely outside the circle of weapon-throwers. He seemed sad and
forgotten, and he hung his head in a pitiful way. It was
Höd, the blind brother of Balder.

The old woman touched his arm. "Why do you not join
the game with the others?" she asked, in her cracked
voice. "Are you the only one to do your brother no honor?
Surely, you are big and strong enough to toss a spear with
the best of them yonder."

Höd touched his sightless eyes madly. "I am blind," he
said. "Strength I have, greater than belongs to most of the
Æsir. But I cannot see to aim a weapon. Besides, I have no
spear to test upon him. Yet how gladly would I do honor
to dear Balder!" and he sighed deeply.

"It were a pity if I could not find you at least a little stick
to throw," said Loki sympathetically. "I am only a poor old
woman, and of course I have no weapon. But ah,—here is
a green twig which you can use as an arrow, and I will
guide your arm, poor fellow."

Höd's dark face lighted up, for he was eager to take his
turn in the game. So he thanked her, and grasped eagerly
the little arrow which she put into his hand. Loki held him
by the arm, and together they stepped into the circle
which surrounded Balder. And when it was Höd's turn to
throw his weapon, the old woman stood at his elbow and
guided his big arm as it hurled the twig of mistletoe
towards where Balder stood.

Oh, the sad thing that befell! Straight through the air
flew the little arrow, straight as magic and Loki's arm
could direct it. Straight to Balder's heart it sped, piercing
through jerkin and shirt and all, to give its bitter message
of "Loki's love," as he had said. With a cry Balder fell for-

ward on the grass. And that was the end of sunshine and spring and joy in Asgard, for the dream had come true, and Balder the beautiful was dead.

When the Æsir saw what had happened, there was a great shout of fear and horror, and they rushed upon Höd, who had thrown the fatal arrow.

"What is it? What have I done?" asked the poor blind brother, trembling at the tumult which had followed his shot.

"You have slain Balder!" cried the Æsir. "Wretched Höd, how could you do it?"

"It was the old woman—the evil old woman, who stood at my elbow and gave me a little twig to throw," gasped Höd. "She must be a witch."

Then the Æsir scattered over Ida Plain to look for the old woman who had done the evil deed; but she had mysteriously disappeared.

"It must be Loki," said wise Heimdal. "It is Loki's last and vilest trick."

"Oh, my Balder, my beautiful Balder!" wailed Queen Frigg, throwing herself on the body of her son. "If I had only made the mistletoe give me the promise, you would have been saved. It was I who told Loki of the mistletoe,— so it is I who have killed you. Oh, my son, my son!"

But Father Odin was speechless with grief. His sorrow was greater than that of all the others, for he best understood the dreadful misfortune which had befallen Asgard. Already a cloud had come before the sun, so that it would never be bright day again. Already the flowers had begun to fade and the birds had ceased to sing. And already the Æsir had begun to grow old and joyless,—all because the little mistletoe had been too young to give a promise to Queen Frigg.

"Balder the beautiful is dead!" the cry went echoing through all the world, and everything that was sorrowed at the sound of the Æsir's weeping.

Balder's brothers lifted up his beautiful body upon their

great war shields and bore him on their shoulders down
to the seashore. For, as was the custom in those days,
they were going to send him to Hela, the Queen of Death,
with all the things he best had loved in Asgard. And these
were,— after Nanna his wife,—his beautiful horse, and his
ship Hringhorni. So that they would place Balder's body
upon the ship with his horse beside him, and set fire to
this wonderful funeral pile. For by fire was the quickest
passage to Hela's kingdom.

But when they reached the shore, they found that all
the strength of all the Æsir was unable to move
Hringhorni, Balder's ship, into the water. For it was the
largest ship in the world, and it was stranded far up the
beach.

"Even the giants bore no ill-will to Balder," said Father
Odin. "I heard the thunder of their grief but now shaking
the hills. Let us for this once bury our hatred of that race
and send to Jotunheim for help to move the ship."

So they sent a messenger to the giantess Hyrrockin, the
hugest of all the Frost People. She was weeping for Balder
when the message came.

"I will go, for Balder's sake," she said. Soon she came
riding fast upon a giant wolf, with a serpent for the bridle;
and mighty she was, with the strength of forty Æsir. She
dismounted from her wolf-steed, and tossed the wriggling reins to one of the men-heroes who had followed
Balder and the Æsir from Valhalla. But he could not hold
the beast, and it took four heroes to keep him quiet,
which they could only do by throwing him upon the
ground and sitting upon him in a row. And this mortified
them greatly.

Then Hyrrockin the giantess strode up to the great ship
and seized it by the prow. Easily she gave a little pull and
presto! it leaped forward on its rollers with such force
that sparks flew from the flint stones underneath and the
whole earth trembled. The boat shot into the waves and
out toward open sea so swiftly that the Æsir were likely to

have lost it entirely, had not Hyrrockin waded out up to her waist and caught it by the stern just in time.

Thor was angry at her clumsiness, and raised his hammer to punish her. But the other Æsir held his arm. "She cannot help being so strong," they whispered. "She meant to do well. She did not realize how hard she was pulling. This is no time for anger, brother Thor." So Thor spared her life, as indeed he ought, for her kindness.

Then Balder's body was borne out to the ship and laid upon a pile of beautiful silks, and furs, and cloth-of-gold, and woven sunbeams which the dwarfs had wrought. So that his funeral pyre was more grand than anything which had ever been seen. But when Nanna, Balder's gentle wife, saw them ready to kindle the flames under this gorgeous bed, she could bear her grief no longer. Her loving heart broke, and they laid her beside him, that they might comfort each other on their journey to Hela. Thor touched the pile gently with his hammer that makes the lightning, and the flames burst forth, lighting up the faces of Balder and Nanna with a glory. Then they cast upon the fire Balder's war-horse, to serve his master in the dark country to which he was about to go. The horse was decked with a harness all of gold, with jewels studding the bridle and headstall. Last of all Odin laid upon the pyre his gift to Balder, Draupnir, the precious ring of gold which the dwarf had made, from which every ninth night there dropped eight other rings as large and brightly golden.

"Take this with you, dear son, to Hela's palace," said Odin. "And do not forget the friends you leave behind in the now lonely halls of Asgard."

Then Hyrrockin pushed the great boat out to sea, with its bonfire of precious things. And on the beach stood all the Æsir watching it out of sight, all the Æsir and many besides. For there came to Balder's funeral great crowds of little dwarfs and multitudes of huge frost giants, all mourning for Balder the beautiful. For this one time they were all friends together, forgetting their quarrels of so many centuries. All of them loved Balder, and were united to do him honor.

The great ship moved slowly out to sea, sending up a red fire to color all the heavens. At last it slid below the horizon softly, as you have often seen the sun set upon the water, leaving a brightness behind to lighten the dark world for a little while.

This indeed was the sunset for Asgard. The darkness of sorrow came in earnest after the passing of Balder the beautiful.

But the punishment of Loki was a terrible thing. And that came soon and sore.

The Punishment of Loki

After the death of Balder the world grew so dreary that no one had any heart left for work or play. The Æsir sat about moping and miserable. They were growing old,—there was no doubt about that. There was no longer any gladness in Valhalla, where the Valkyries waited on table and poured the foaming mead. There was no longer any mirth on Ida Plain, when every morning the bravest of earth-heroes fought their battles over again. Odin no longer had any pleasure in the daily news brought by his wise ravens, Thought and Memory, nor did Freia enjoy her falcon dress. Frey forgot to sail in his ship Skidbladnir, and even Thor had almost wearied of his hammer, except as he hoped that it would help him to catch Loki. For the one thought of all of them now was to find and punish Loki.

Yet they waited; for Queen Frigg had sent a messenger to Queen Hela to find if they might not even yet win Balder back from the kingdom of death.

Odin shook his head. "Queen Hela is Loki's daughter," he said, "and she will not let Balder return." But Frigg was hopeful; she had employed a trusty messenger, whose silver tongue had won many hearts against their will.

It was Hermod, Balder's brother, who galloped down the steep road to Hela's kingdom, on Sleipnir, the eight-legged horse of Father Odin. For nine nights and nine days he rode, through valleys dark and chill, until he came to the bridge which is paved with gold. And here the maiden Modgard told him that Balder had passed that way, and showed him the path northward to Hela's city. So he rode, down and

down, until he came to the high wall which surrounded the
grim palace where Hela reigned. Hermod dismounted and
tightened the saddle-girths of gray Sleipnir, whose eight legs
were as frisky as ever, despite the long journey. And when
he had mounted once more, the wonderful horse leaped
with him over the wall, twenty feet at least!

Then Hermod rode straight into the palace of Hela,
straight up to the throne where she sat surrounded by
gray shadows and spirit people. She was a dreadful creature to see, was this daughter of Loki,—half white like
other folk, but half black, which was not sunburn, for
there was no sunshine in this dark and dismal land. Yet
she was not so bad as she looked; for even Hela felt kindly
towards Balder, whom her father had slain, and was sorry
that the world had lost so dear a friend. So when Hermod
begged of her to let his brother return with him to Asgard,
she said very gently,—

"Freely would I let him go, brave Hermod, if I might. But
a queen cannot always do as she likes, even in her own
kingdom. His life must be bought; the price must be paid
in tears. If everything upon earth will weep for Balder's
death, then may he return, bringing light and happiness to
the upper world. Should one creature fail to weep, Balder
must remain with me."

Then Hermod was glad, for he felt sure that this price
was easily paid. He thanked Hela, and made ready to
depart with the hopeful message. Before he went away he
saw and spoke with Balder himself, who sat with Nanna
upon a throne of honor, talking of the good times that
used to be. And Balder gave him the ring Draupnir to give
back to Father Odin, as a remembrance from his dear son;
while Nanna sent to mother Frigg her silver veil with other
rich presents. It was hard for Hermod to part with Balder
once again, and Balder also wept to see him go. But
Hermod was in duty bound to bear the message back to
Asgard as swiftly as might be.

Now when the Æsir heard from Hermod this news, they
sent messengers forth over the whole world to bid every

creature weep for Balder's death. Heimdal galloped off upon Goldtop and Frey upon Goldbristle, his famous hog; Thor rumbled away in his goat chariot, and Freia drove her team of cats,—all spreading the message in one direction and another. There really seemed little need for them to do this, for already there was mourning in every land and clime. Even the sky was weeping, and the flower eyes were filled with dewy tears.

So it seemed likely that Balder would be ransomed after all, and the Æsir began to hope more strongly. For they had not found one creature who refused to weep. Even the giants of Jotunheim were sorry to lose the gentle fellow who had never done them any harm, and freely added their giant tears to the salt rivers that were coursing over all the world into the sea, making it still more salt.

It was not until the messengers had nearly reached home, joyful in the surety that Balder was safe, that they found an ugly old giantess named Thökt hidden in a black cavern among the mountains.

"Weep, mother, weep for Balder!" they cried. "Balder the beautiful is dead, but your tears will buy him back to life. Weep, mother, weep!"

But the sulky old woman refused to weep.

"Balder is nothing to me," she said. "I care not whether he lives or dies. Let him bide with Hela—he is out of mischief there. I weep dry tears for Balder's death."

So all the work of the messengers was in vain, because of this one obstinate old woman. So all the tears of the sorrowing world were shed in vain. Because there were lacking two salty drops from the eyes of Thökt, they could not buy back Balder from the prison of death.

When the messengers returned and told Odin their sad news, he was wrathful.

"Do you not guess who the old woman was?" he cried. "It was Loki—Loki himself, disguised as a giantess. He has tricked us once more, and for a second time has slain Balder for us; for it is now too late,—Balder can never return to us after this. But it shall be the last of Loki's mischief. It is now time that we put an end to his deeds of shame."

"Come, my brothers!" shouted Thor, flourishing his hammer. "We have wept and mourned long enough. It is now time to punish. Let us hasten back to Thökt's cave, and seize Loki as quickly as may be."

So they hurried back into the mountains where they had left the giantess who would not weep. But when they came to the place, the cave was empty. Loki was too sharp a fellow to sit still and wait for punishment to overtake him. He knew very well that the Æsir would soon discover who Thökt really was. And he had taken himself off to a safer place, to escape the questions which a whole world of not too gentle folk were anxious to ask him.

The one desire of the Æsir was now to seize and punish Loki. So when they were unable to find him as easily as they expected, they were wroth indeed. Why had he left the cave? Whither had he gone? In what new disguise even now was he lurking, perhaps close by?

The truth was that when Loki found himself at war with the whole world which he had injured, he fled away into the mountains, where he had built a strong castle of rocks. This castle had four doors, one looking into the north, one to the south, one to the east, and one to the west; so that Loki could keep watch in all directions and see any enemy who might approach. Besides this, he had for his protection the many disguises which he knew so well how to don. Near the castle was a river and a waterfall, and it was Loki's favorite game to change himself into a spotted pink salmon and splash about in the pool below the fall.

"Ho, ho! Let them try to catch me here, if they can!" he would chuckle to himself. And indeed, it seemed as if he were safe enough.

One day Loki was sitting before the fire in his castle twisting together threads of flax and yarn into a great fish-net which was his own invention. For no one had ever before thought of catching fish with a net. Loki was a clever fellow; and with all his faults, for this one thing at least the fishermen of to-day ought to be grateful to him. As Loki sat busily knotting the meshes of the net, he happened to glance out of the south door,—and there were the Æsir coming in a body up the hill towards his castle.

Now this is what had happened: from his lookout throne in Asgard, Odin's keen sight had spied Loki's retreat. This throne, you remember, was in the house with a silver roof which Odin had built in the very beginning of time; and whenever he wanted to see what was going on in the remotest corner of Asgard, or to spy into some secret place beyond the sight of gods or men, he would mount this magic throne, whence his eye could pierce thick mountains and sound the deepest sea. So it was that the Æsir had found out Loki's castle, well-hidden though it was among the furthest mountains of the world. They had come to catch him, and there was nothing left for him but to run.

Loki jumped up and threw his half-mended net into the fire, for he did not want the Æsir to discover his invention; then he ran down to the river and leaped in with a great splash. When he was well under water, he changed himself into a salmon, and flickered away to bask in his shady pool and think how safe he was.

By this time the Æsir had entered his castle and were poking among the ashes which they found smouldering on the hearth.

"What is this?" asked Thor, holding up a piece of knotted flax which was not quite burned. "The knave has been making something with little cords."

"Let me see it," said Heimdal, the wisest of the Æsir,—he who once upon a time had suggested Thor's clever disguise for winning back his hammer from the giant Thrym. He took now the little scrap of fish-net and studied it carefully, picking out all the knots and twists of it.

"It is a net," said Heimdal at last. "He has been making a net, and—pfaugh!—it smells of fish. The fellow must have used it to trap fish for his dinner, though I never before heard of such a device."

"I saw a big splash in the river just as we came up," said Thor the keen-eyed,—"a very big splash indeed. It seemed too large for any fish."

"It was Loki," declared Heimdal. "He must have been here but a moment since, for this fire has just gone out, and the net is still smouldering. That shows he did not wish us to find this new-fangled idea of his. Why was that? Let me think. Aha! I have it. Loki has changed himself into a fish, and did not wish us to discover the means of catching him."

"Oho!" cried the Æsir regretfully. "If only we had another net!"

"We can make one," said wise Heimdal. "I know how it is done, for I have studied out this little sample. Let us make a net to catch the slyest of all fish."

"Let us make a net for Loki," echoed the Æsir. And they all sat down cross-legged on the floor to have a lesson in net-weaving from Heimdal. He found hemp cord in a cupboard, and soon they had contrived a goodly net, big enough to catch several Lokis, if they should have good fisherman's luck.

They dragged the net to the river and cast it in. Thor, being the strongest, held one end of the net, and all the rest drew the other end up and down the stream. They were clumsy and awkward, for they had never used a net before, and did not know how to make the best of it. But presently Thor exclaimed, "Ha! I felt some live thing touch the meshes!"

"So did we!" cried the others. "It must be Loki!" And Loki it was, sure enough; for the Æsir had happened upon the very pool where the great salmon lay basking so peacefully. But when he felt the net touch him, he darted away and hid in a cleft between two rocks. So that, although they dragged the net to and fro again and again, they could not catch Loki in its meshes; for the net was so light that it floated over his head.

"We must weight the net," said Heimdal wisely; "then nothing can pass beneath it." So they tied heavy stones all along the under edge, and again they cast the net, a little below the waterfall. Now Loki had seized the chance to swim further down the stream. But ugh! suddenly he tasted salt water. He was being swept out to sea! That would never do, for he could not live an hour in the sea. So he swam back and leaped straight over the net up into the waterfall, hoping that no one had noticed him. But Thor's sharp eyes had spied the flash of pink and silver, and Thor came running to the place.

"He is here!" he shouted. "Cast in the net above the fall! We have him now!"

When Loki saw the net cast again, so that there was no choice for him but to be swept back over the falls and out to sea, or to leap the net once more still further up the river, he hesitated. He saw Thor in the middle of the stream wading towards him; but behind him was sure death. So he set his teeth and once more he leaped the net. There was a huge splash, a scuffle, a scramble, and the water was churned into froth all about Thor's feet. He was struggling with the mighty fish. He caught him once, but the salmon slipped through his fingers. He caught him again, and this time Thor gripped hard. The salmon almost escaped, but Thor's big fingers kept hold of the end of his tail, and he flapped and flopped in vain. It was the grip of Thor's iron glove; and that is why to this day the salmon has so pointed a tail. The next time you see a salmon you must notice this, and remember that he may be a great-great-great-grand-descendant of Loki.

So Loki was captured and changed back into his own shape, sullen and fierce. But he had no word of sorrow for his evil deeds; nor did he ask for mercy, for he knew that it would be in vain. He kept silent while the Æsir led him all the weary way back to Asgard.

Now the whole world was noisy with the triumph of his capture. As the procession passed along it was joined by all the creatures who had mourned for Balder,—all the creatures who longed to see Loki punished. There were the men of Midgard, the place of human folk, shouting, "Kill him! Kill him!" at the top of their lungs; there were armies of little mountain dwarfs in their brown peaked caps, who hobbled along, prodding Loki with their picks; there were beasts growling and showing their teeth as if they longed to tear Loki in pieces; there were birds who tried to peck his eyes, insects who came in clouds to sting him, and serpents that sprang up hissing at his feet to poison him with their deadly bite.

But to all these Thor said, "Do not kill the fellow. We are keeping him for a worse punishment than you can give." So the creatures merely followed and jostled Loki into Asgard, shouting, screaming, howling, growling, barking, roaring, spitting, squeaking, hissing, croaking, and buzzing, according to their different ways of showing hatred and horror.

The Æsir met on Ida Plain to decide what should be done with Loki. There were Idun whom he had cheated, and Sif whose hair he had cut off. There were Freia whose falcon dress he had stolen and Thor whom he had tried to kill. There were Höd whom he had made a murderer; Frigg and Odin whose son he had slain. There was not one of them whom Loki had not injured in some way; and besides, there was the whole world into which he had brought sorrow and darkness; for the sake of all these Loki must be punished. But it was hard to think of any doom heavy enough for him. At last, however, they agreed upon a punishment which they thought suited to so wicked a wretch.

The long procession formed again and escorted Loki down, down into a damp cavern underground. Here sunlight never came, but the cave was full of ugly toads, snakes, and insects that love the dark. These were Loki's evil thoughts, who were to live with him henceforth and torment him always. In this prison chamber side by side they placed three sharp stones, not far apart, to make an uneasy bed. And these were for Loki's three worst deeds,

"Kill him! Kill him!"
See page 146.

against Thor and Höd and Balder. Upon these rocks they bound Loki with stout thongs of leather. But as soon as the cords were fastened they turned into iron bands, so that no one, though he had the strength of a hundred giants, could loosen them. For these were Loki's evil passions, and the more he strained against them, the more they cut into him and wounded him until he howled with pain.

Over his head Skadi, whose father he had helped to slay, hung a venomous, wriggling serpent, from whose mouth dropped poison into Loki's face, which burned and stung him like fire. And this was the deceit which all his life Loki had spoken to draw folk into trouble and danger. At last it had turned about to torture him, as deceit always will do to him who utters it. Yet from this one torment Loki had some relief; for alone of all the world Sigyn, his wife, was faithful and forgiving. She stood by the head of the painful bed upon which the Red One was stretched, and held a bowl to catch the poison which dropped from the serpent's jaws, so that some of it did not reach Loki's face. But as often as the bowl became full, Sigyn had to go out and empty it; and then the bitter drops fell and burned till Loki made the cavern ring with his cries.

So this was Loki's punishment, and bad enough it was,— but not too bad for such a monster. Under the caverns he lies there still, struggling to be free. And when his great strength shakes the hills so that the whole ground trembles, men call it an earthquake. Sometimes they even see his poisonous breath blowing from the top of a mountain-chimney, and amid it the red flame of wickedness which burns in Loki's heart. Then all cry, "The volcano, the volcano!" and run away as fast as they can. For Loki, poisoned though he is, is still dangerous and full of mischief, and it is not good to venture near him in his torment.

But there for his sins he must bide and suffer, suffer and bide, until the end of all sorrow and suffering and sin shall come, with Ragnarök, the ending of the world.